MODERN
SHORT STORIES

Ezra Dangoor

Grosvenor House
Publishing Limited

This book is published by
Grosvenor House Publishing Ltd
Link House
140 The Broadway, Tolworth, Surrey, Kt6 7Ht.
www.grosvenorhousepublishing.co.uk

A CIP record for this book
is available from the British Library

ISBN 978-1-78623-794-1

SYNOPSIS

Most of my short stories are factual, while some are not.

I left the academic world in 1980 upon coming to England and got engrossed in the business world, leaving "the road less travelled by."

While on the job, I started writing bits and pieces to pass the time. I did not make a conscious effort to write but rather jotted down what came to my mind in bits and pieces.

I felt compelled to write down events that occurred which, as I mentioned in one of my stories, reminded me of the Ancient Mariner. A good example is the story of "Elias" which leaves me with a lasting memory.

On the fictitious side, what seems to be fiction today, will prove to be fact in some distant future. Basically, I believe in three things:

Firstly, just as we came to this planet, we shall definitely be recreated somewhere else.

Secondly, a time factor is to be considered. We might be "created" billions of "years" in the future as we now know it or billions of years in the "past."

Thirdly, the physical shape, or even the unit of energy, into which we will be created will depend on where we will be destined to be "created."

Thus, what now seems to us to be Science Fiction today, may well prove to be fact in the "future."

E. Dangoor

AUTOBIOGRAPHY

Most readers do not like to read autobiographies, unless they are by very famous authors. So, I will make mine as brief as possible.

I was born in Tehran, Iran on August 28, 1944.

I attended the Presbyterian Mission School in Tehran, from where I graduated in 1962.

In Sept 1962, I attended Fairleigh Dickinson University in Madison, New Jersey, from where I graduated in 1966 receiving a BA degree in Liberal Arts in 1966. I continued my studies at the University of Michigan, receiving an MA degree in literature in 1967. Although I got an acceptance to study for a PHD degree at New York University, I was unable to attend as I had to go back and visit my family in Tehran.

I taught English language and literature as an assistant professor at the National University of Iran from 1967 to 1980.

I arrived in London in 1980 and worked as an electrical wholesaler in various areas of the city until my retirement in December 1015.

Ezra Dangoor

July 2016

CONTENTS

THE HUDDLE
OF HUMANITY

Elena Birdachevsky stood dazed in the balcony of her first floor flat as the two men she had had in her life came back to her in a flashback of a dream.

She had married her husband Roger at the age of 18 "out of love." He was the first man in her life and she had had no experience of being with or even seeing another man. So, what did love mean to her? Perhaps it was the fascination of being with an athlete of a man, a man with a perfect physical build, a Paris of a man who exists only in fairy tales, mythologies, and dreams.

But this marriage could not last, would not last. For one thing, her prince charming lacked the means that could bring her more than the basic comforts of life. He was only a salaried trainer in a health club. For another, she was getting disenchanted with this "love" which was supposed to happen at marriage and gradually evolve from the physical to the spiritual. Her husband was not spiritually inclined and couldn't understand these things. For him "love" was sex and that was all there was to it. She was looking for the type of "love" that she had read about in the sonnets of Shakespeare or the poems of John Donne and that would never be.

He claimed that he passionately loved her. But to her, he was a mere, sensual animal. He would come home, eat and drink whatever was laid on the table, make love, watch some news on the TV and then go to bed. There was nothing to talk about or discuss that had any depth.

What was of utmost importance to him was his health. He must have been a hypochondriac. "If my health goes," he would say, "then how will we survive?" He kept on talking about his diet and what would be the best foods for him. He needed to eat organic foods. "Fruits and vegetables are full of pesticides," he would say. "Meat contains cholesterol and even fish is not safe, what with the pollution of the seas and oceans with human and industrial waste."

He needed to exercise every day. Even on holidays, he would go to the gym, spending hours there. He claimed that the pollution in the city was destroying his health and that he didn't have the means to go live in the country.

For eight years she had had to put up with him. What about her needs? Never once had he asked her how she felt or what was lacking in her life. He was not concerned.

She remembered that once when she had fallen ill with the flu, she had had to nurse herself back to health. Except for a "hello" or "goodbye," she was completely ignored. She confined herself to a separate room as Roger was afraid of catching the flu from her. So, she had had to make her own food and stay in her room when Roger returned from work. When she asked him to fetch some medicines for her from the local pharmacy, he replied that people had to rely on their own natural defences rather than on drugs. But he did buy her some orange juice and canned soups though. So, where was that "love" and where was "compassion?"

She desperately wanted a family. Every time she saw children playing in the streets or neighbours taking the babies out in a pram, her motherly instincts would swell within her.

After eight years of marriage, she started contemplating divorce. But how could she bring up the subject? It had become a "do I dare and do I dare" question. She had to pop the question at the right time, perhaps at a time when he would show some dissatisfaction with her. This would probably alleviate the tension and distress which would be too overpowering when the question had to be asked.

It was all her mother's fault. Helena hated her daughter with a passion which was nowhere natural or motherly. She had made all the necessary arrangements for daughter to meet Roger and did everything possible to get them hitched. She wanted Elena out of the house, out of her life. She nagged and nagged and nagged. "Don't you want a life of your own?" "Girls at the age of 14 are already married and with child."

Helena's love for her children had dried up, dried up as milk dries up in the breasts of an unfeeding mother. It had dried up with the untimely death of her husband who had died at the age of 55 from a stroke and had left her alone to face the world with no income. She recalled how hard she had had to work to trap and dominate the professor of a husband she had so admired. With his death, she had had to hold various jobs, no matter how demeaning, to bring up the children. In their house there was always tension, a grinding tension that seemed to put them all against each other and wear them down. Elena tried to stay as distant and aloof from her mother as possible. Her sister, on the other hand, begged and pleaded with her mother in her attempts to suck the last drops of motherly love that may have remained in her mother's bosom.

Finally, one evening Elena felt that the moment was ripe for her to pop the question. Roger had come home and she had served him with the usual bowl of vegetable soup which she had so methodically prepared. He muttered under his breath but she was used to this. Something about the soup not containing the proper vegetables and its being too watery. He went on to grumble that as a result of her cooking, his health was deteriorating.

"Well," she thought to herself. "If this isn't the right moment to pop the question, then I won't know when it will be." She wondered what kind of reaction to expect. Would there be a volcanic eruption of anger at her having dared? Would he passionately declare his love for her even though there was no trace of it? Or would he simply entreat her, beg her to stay and give him another chance.

She decided not to "turn back and descend the stair" no matter what. She pulled up her chair to face her husband and sat down waiting for him to lift his head so that she could look him in the eyes when asking the question. The eyes, they say, are the portholes to the soul she thought. I have to make sure that I look deep into his eyes so as to capture his innermost feelings.

Aware of her presence, Roger lifted his head and looked at her with an empty stare. Underneath the table, she clenched her left hand with the right, squeezing it hard so as to gather the courage as she blurted out "I think we should get divorced."

There were only a few moments of silence. It was as though Roger was expecting the question. His cold response was "If you so wish."

II

They met in the lawyer's office. Roger offered half of their possessions which consisted of a double bed, a sofa, a dining room table which was not much to talk about, four chairs and, of course, the kitchenware. Elena decided that she didn't want anything. She had packed a small suitcase of clothes and had brought it with her to avoid returning to the flat.

What was she to do now with $100 and some change in her pocket and with no one to turn to? Her first priority was to find a place to sleep at night. She most certainly couldn't stay in the streets. Once you start sleeping in the streets, you plummet.......plop, plop, plop, plop....And there's no bottom.

As she had not been out of the flat much, she had no friends and no one to turn to. She would not consider going to her mother for she would not be able to withstand her abuses and sarcasm. This would be worse than sleeping rough.

Then she remembered the old man who lived in the flat below hers. He was in his seventies with silver hair. He was quite polite and would ask her about her health and whether everything was okay with her. As far as she knew, he was single and perhaps he would let her sleep on his sofa for a few nights until she could figure out what to do.

She had nothing to lose by asking. But she also remembered that she could feel lust in his eyes whenever she met him outside the flats. She also felt that every time she would turn around to leave, his lusty glare would burn a hole in her buttocks. But what the hell. She was a good looking woman and many heads would turn when she walked in the streets or shopped in the supermarket. She was slender, five foot eight, and a self- made blonde with hair hanging to her shoulders.

George was very verbose and nor did he have a good memory. He kept recounting his life story and never knew when to stop. She had tolerated him no matter how many times he repeated his life story. Sometimes she would go up and get him a cup of coffee and some cookies as she had had a lot of time on her hands.

George had lost all his money in the property market. He was a builder but wanted to build Gaudi-like buildings. He believed that he was way ahead of his times in building design. He had had a difficult time selling his flats and, as a result, the banks closed in on him.

When he was at the height of his fortunes, he commanded a lot of respect, especially from his family. He had owned a country home where the family would retreat on the weekends and where his friends and relatives would gather. There were no invitations. All who came were welcome. A lamb would be slaughtered and prepared for barbecue. His loving wife was always by his side, catering to his every wish. His children did everything they could to please him. What else could a man wish for?

But things went sour when the courts bankrupted him. His children distanced themselves from him as one would from a leper. If his name came up in social circles where they were present, they acted as if their father was a stranger. And most of all, his loving wife started hating him with a passion.

She lost all respect for him. They quarrelled every day. George tried to keep the peace at any cost but it was useless.

In response to his being passive, she became aggressive. Elena often heard their outbursts of anger and she recalled that once she had also heard the noise of breaking cutlery. They must have separated soon afterwards as Elena no longer saw his wife.

Elena returned to the flats and placed her small suitcase by the entrance outside George's flat, waiting for George. He was her only hope and she wished that she had been more social and attentive to him. But she had not ignored him. She had been a married woman and she was sure he was quite aware of that.

Should worse come to worse, she thought, she would have to spend a few weeks in the airport lounges. There, she would be out of harm's way and she could also use the toilet facilities.

At about 5:30 pm George appeared. He looked rugged and old. Elena guessed that he was in his late sixties or early seventies. He had a headful of white hair and was wearing muddied shoes and paint stained grey trousers that were held up by shoulder straps meant to accommodate his bulging stomach. His face looked gloomy and burdened, suggesting that the wrinkles of a smile were foreign to his face.

A glimmer came to his face when he saw Elena sitting on the steps. He thought that she was probably waiting to ask him something. Or maybe she was anxiously waiting her husband's return and had been locked out. In any case, even these brief encounters were a source of joy to him.

Elena did not exactly know how she could pose the question she wanted to ask. She knew that George had some idea that she and her husband were not getting along well. Many a times, she had hinted that she was having trouble with her relationship. George was not stupid either. He looked at the little suitcase:

"Are you going on a holiday?"

"Not really. Probably you are aware that we were having problems."

"Yes, sort of."

"Well, we got divorced today and I waited to tell you goodbye."

"You're staying with relatives, I suppose."

Tears rolled down her cheeks but she didn't bother to wipe them off. She believed that George must have a soft spot somewhere within him. At the same time, she knew that he was attracted to her physically. So, she tried to entice him by concocting these two feelings within him.

She stood up and bent down to pick up her suitcase, making sure that George could see the part of her thighs that the raised dress would reveal.

"I don't have anywhere to go to," she said in a somewhat seductive tone.

"You could stay with me for a while. I have an extra sofa in the living room."

It was quite a relief for Elena. She was quite aware of what she was doing. If she could add some spice to his dull life, she could mould him like putty in her hands.

George was not a professional builder. He would do small jobs like plastering and painting etc. but whatever job he was given, he did it quite well. So, he was in demand and managed to pay his rent and make a living as well.

As Elena had nothing to do, George asked her if she would like to be his assistant. He explained that he couldn't pay her much and that she would have to get an evening job to supplement her income.

He taught her how to undercoat and paint and she was happy doing that. She didn't mind the little pay as she was not paying George any rent but soon she would have to find her own accommodation. So she saved every penny George gave her.

At the present, she would have to keep George happy on the job but, most important, she would have to add some spice to his life. In short, that would be the spark that would keep him going. And this came naturally to her. For example, she would massage his shoulders after dinner. She would wear short skirts at work and arouse him as she climbed the ladder. Little things like that.

But the motherly instincts of having children kept on creeping upon her and grinding her guts. The grinding was wearing her out. She simply had to find a partner by hook or by crook. She was not particular any more. Any decent chap would do.

III

Eventually, Elena found a part-time job in a restaurant as a waitress. She worked there on the weekends, taking orders, serving the customers and also cleaning the tables. It was hard work but the pay was good and she would have the opportunity to meet people.

Having saved some money, Elena asked George if he could find her a room that she could rent. She wanted her independence and what if she were to find a gentleman that she could invite over? After a while George was also happy to let her go. So he found her a room that had previously been used as storage in a building nearby.

He partitioned the room and put in a second-hand toilet and shower. He couldn't find a second- hand bed so he sorted her out with a mattress and a pillow. He also got her an electric oil filled radiator for the heating.

They were both content but they didn't have much to look forward to. They lived each day as it came, and they tried to make the most of it. A sandwich and a drink would suffice for lunch. Sometimes, if business was good, George would take Elena for a coffee and a cake after work in one of the outdoor cafes. Perhaps they were blessed, at least for a while. For, this leisure that came upon them as a result of their modest life also brought a very small degree of awareness of the pleasures and beauty of life, even though they may not have fully realized it.

It didn't take much to make George happy. He believed that what would come would come, no use struggling to make more. With his situation, he would never become rich and he was resigned to this fact. As long as he had a little money in his pocket, he was content to live out his life. He would never stop working as he equated idleness with death. Once you are idle, you start dying.

As for Elena, she believed that she was still young, but not too young. She believed that at the age of 26, she didn't have much time to bear healthy children. Her genetic build-up would prevent this. Thirty was the limit and she had to do something about it.

She would have to be outgoing and aggressive. She had to make the first move in order to secure a companion. Otherwise, life would pass her by. She would not let any opportunity escape her. She would approach any man she thought could be a potential husband or even companion to father children.

And so it came to pass that one day she met someone at the checkout of the supermarket. She was carrying a basket of food while the man in front of her had a loaded trolley.

"You may stand in front of me if you wish as you only have a few items."

"That's awfully nice of you," she replied.

He wasn't particularly handsome, but if he was a bachelor, he would do. He was tall, slim, with short cropped hair and seemed to be in his early forties. She thought his accent was Spanish. There was nothing to lose, so she decided to have a go.

"You must have plenty of mouths to feed," she chuckled.

"Not at all. I have a big fridge-freezer and I shop once a week. I hate shopping."

"Then you must be single, like me as it seems that you do your own shopping." She specially put that bit about her being single to find out what his response might be.

"If I was married, I would never shop for food. This is a woman's job."

She paid for her purchases but lingered as he put his groceries in bags and back into the trolley.

"May I help you with the packing?"

"That' all right. I'm almost finished."

There was not much time left now as indeed he was almost finished. For whatever reason, she felt that he would never ask for a date so she blurted out the question. She had nothing to lose.

"Would you like to meet for a coffee sometime?"

"Can't make it today but what about tomorrow lunchtime? At the El Passo Restaurant? Do you know where it is?"

"Of course. Everyone knows where it is. What time?"

"Anytime you wish. My work schedule is flexible. How about 2 pm. It's less busy then."

"It's a date," she said and walked off.

As she walked to her flat, she realized that they hadn't even exchanged names. How stupid of her. But even he hadn't asked her name. Perhaps he didn't care as this could not slip a man's mind .Many thoughts passed through her mind. She still didn't know whether he was married or not but she would soon find out, that is, if he were to show up. But why was his work schedule "flexible?" His attire did not suggest that he was wealthy, but rather middle class. And the "El Passo" Restaurant? She wasn't superstitious but that name suggested something ominous. It certainly didn't imply a lasting relationship, only a fleeting one.

Elena left her flat at 1:30 pm the following day. I would take her about a half hour to reach the coffee shop by subway but she wanted to be about 10 to 15 minutes late. This way, she could just leave if he was not there waiting.

Walking toward the restaurant, she saw him pacing by the front entrance.

"I'm sorry to be a few minutes late," she said as she approached him. "In my excitement, I didn't even ask your name."

"Nor did I, but I figured that you would show up if you were interested."

They were led to a table by the window overlooking the street and ordered their coffees and cakes.

"You know, at the supermarket we were in such a hurry that I even forgot to ask your name, or to give you mine, " she reiterated excitedly.

"My name if Paul, or maybe Sir Paul, if you wish to regard me as an aristocrat," he said teasingly.

"Your highness, my name is Elena, or Cinderella, if you so wish. Perhaps we should have met just before midnight. And does Sir Paul have a constant entourage?"

"Unfortunately Sir Paul leads a lonely life. In short, he is a bachelor and lives alone."

"And what is Sir Paul's profession, if I may ask? I was wondering as you said you could meet me anytime."

"I consider myself to be a poet. I write when inspiration gets hold of me, that is when the muses are not busy and they respond which is not that often. At other times, I do translations here and there to make enough money to survive."

"That's an interesting way of life, especially if you have money. You could always be travelling to exotic and distant places, meet different people with various cultures and entice your palette with gourmet dishes."

"But in my case it's not so as I don't have much savings. I can't really travel as I live from the translation work I do."

IV

Elena kept seeing Paul and eventually invited him to live with her. At least she would have a companion to come back to and spend the nights with and, more important, she was hoping that the relationship would develop and someday she could be with child from him.

As time passed, she found out that Paul had been a loner whose only income was from the few translation works he would do and which were from English to Spanish and vice versa. She found out that when he had been living on his own, he would only leave his flat once a week to do some shopping but now that he was living with her he didn't have the need to leave the flat at all. He would work on his computer all day long, eat, drink, rest and wait for her to come home. How can one live without venturing outside? This was bizarre and abnormal as nature is an integral part of life.

Soon he became completely dependent on her. She would have to do the cleaning, washing, and shopping. As he only contributed a little towards the food, she soon found out that she was unable to save anything.

After living with Paul for almost a year, Elena realized that that he didn't care for her much. He was happy with the status quo and all he needed her for was for his comfort and financial security. He wasn't worried about her concern of having children. In fact, he didn't want any. He was a loner who was happy spending months in self- inflicted solitary confinement.

He wasn't concerned that she was working herself to the bone, to get him the basics of life. Sometimes when she would come home, exhausted to the point of collapsing, he would force her to have sex with him. She would take off her clothes and just lie down till he was done.

But he had to give her some kind of hope to keep her going. He told her that he had this rich grandmother living in Spain who was in her early nineties and very sick. She had willed all her possessions to him, including her villa, and her death was imminent. Once she was dead, he promised her a luxurious life style attended by servants, cooks and drivers. It was all a matter of the devil claiming her soul.

Basically, he trusted her but expected her to be punctual. He was not really jealous of anyone she would meet but he didn't want to lose his security. She was his lifeline.

One Saturday night a customer booked a table at the restaurant to celebrate his wife's birthday. They were a group of twenty people and they were not in any hurry to leave. Elena had no choice but to stay till about 2 am when they left. She thought nothing of it as she believed that Paul trusted her and he would certainly understand. Most probably, he would be asleep and she would sneak in, tiptoeing so as not to wake him up.

When she reached the flat she tried to be as quiet as possible but when she pushed the door open, the lights were on and Paul was sitting in the armchair which was facing the door.

"Where the hell have you been?" he queried emphatically.

"There was a party at the restaurant and the customers stayed late."

"This is the second time you have come home late but this time you have overdone it. Tell me, who's the new boyfriend you are fucking, you dirty whore?"

She walked over to him, bent down to his level and looked him in the eyes.

"Here I am slaving away to keep us afloat and now I have to listen to your accusations."

Paul rose to his feet. He was furious.

"I've had enough of you, you whore. I'm going to teach you a lesson you'll never forget."

He clenched his fist and suddenly punched her in the stomach.

She was bent double trying to catch her breath. Fearing he would become more violent, she crossed to the table which stood in one corner of the room and went round it to the far side to avoid him.

But Paul was too quick for her. He leapt behind her and put his arms round the back of her neck in a stranglehold.

"Let me go. You are choking me."

"Perhaps your boyfriend has a gentler touch, bitch."

Elena started screaming and thrustingly lunged forward. As she did so, her forehead hit the edge of the table. Blood started gushing from her head, so much so, that Elena felt faint and fell to the ground. Paul was in a state of shock. He was desperate and didn't know what to do. He quickly brought the Kleenex box and pressed a tissue against her forehead to stop the blood.

He was reluctant to call for an ambulance but had no choice. She was taken to the local hospital and had six stiches put into her forehead.

It was clear to the ambulance crew that there had been a violent confrontation between Elena and Paul and, as a matter of course, they informed the police who arrived at the hospital after Elena had recovered.

Elena found a policeman and a policewoman at her bedside. The policewoman questioned Elena while the policeman took notes.

"You must have lost a lot of blood. Do you feel better?" asked the policewoman.

Elena was very bitter and she was not about to forgive Paul. Her bandaged forehead reminded her of the scars that would remain and for which she would have to save to have plastic surgery done.

"Yes, much better."

"Can you tell us what happened?"

"I came home late and Paul was waiting for me. He thought that I was having an affair. He had positioned his armchair to face the door and as soon as I walked in, he accused me of being unfaithful to him. I suspected his aggression and quickly moved away from him round the table so as to deter him."

Tears swelled in her eyes and flowed down her cheeks.

"Well, it's over now. Don't cry. But maybe you should as it will give vent to your frustrations. What happened then?"

"He was too god damn quick for me. And also there was nowhere to run. I ran across the table but he caught up with me and punched me in the stomach, grabbed me from behind my neck, and pushed my head to the table."

"We have already arrested him for causing grievous bodily harm and if you sign this paper, we shall detain him until there is a court hearing."

Elena signed the paper and Paul was sentenced to six months in prison.

She was now alone. At first she enjoyed her freedom but little by little loneliness started creeping upon her. She could not get rid of this monster who seemed to be destined to become her soulmate if she didn't shake him off. She only had one friend in the restaurant that she could confide in. But Carol was married and had three children and the only time she could share her feelings with her was for the few minutes as they walked to the bus stop.

"Carol, loneliness is killing me. I was not built to have a solitary life. I don't know what to do?"

" It's not only you. Humans are essentially social animals. Why don't you go to a pub or somewhere where you can meet other people?"

"By the time I get home every day, I feel knackered. I don't feel like going anywhere. You know that Paul's been in prison over three months already and I haven't heard a word. Do you think I should visit him?"

"Are you crazy? Paul should be history after what the bastard has done to you and it's not the first time that he has abused you."

"I feel I should forgive him. After all, I've spent almost two years of my life with him."

"Don't kid yourself. He's used you and abused you over and over again. I don't believe this story of his grandmother leaving him all her wealth when she dies. Darling, did you ever see his grandmother?"

1 8

"No."

"Well, I tell you what darling, I'm pretty sure she does not exist. He's just leading you on. That's so you keep on supporting him. Where's the end?"

"I don't what to say or what to think."

"He's created some sort of hope for you just so that he can live off you. Don't you see what he's up to? He's some sort of weirdo. Who can stay in a dark flat day in and day out, never wanting to go out? My advice to you is to get rid of him and now is the best opportunity. Don't let him in again."

"A false hope. Just like a unicorn that doesn't exist."

"A uni what?"

"A unicorn. I read somewhere about this unicorn."

"Whatever, darling."

Every morning, as Elena would look into the mirror to put on her makeup, she would be reminded of the scars that her stiches had created. She was determined to do something about it but she didn't have the money. She made appointments with two different plastic surgeons . One quoted her $2,000 and the other $1,800. There was just no way she could save that kind of money and she had no one to turn to.

She knew that George would not be able to help her as he was practically living from hand to mouth but perhaps he would have some friend who would help.

So, one day as they were leisurely sitting in the sun having their lunch, she decided to ask him. She had nothing to lose.

"George," she said "I don't know what to do with the scars that the stitches have left. It's quite noticeable. Don't you agree?"

"It is noticeable but if someone really likes you, then he won't be worried about it."

"You're right but that is till he gets to know me and like me. But it's the first physical attraction that counts and he is going to be repelled by my looks and probably not approach me at all."

"Well that is true too. It's part of human nature."

"I've been to some surgeons and they are asking about $2,000 to do the plastic surgery. Do you know anyone who would lend me the money? I could pay if off little by little."

"You know that if I personally had it, I would lend you. But I can't think of anyone I know who would lend it to me, not even a few hundred dollars. They ask for security and I have nothing to offer."

"What am I to do, then?"

"For the time being, grow your hair in such a way as to cover the scars on your forehead."

V

Loneliness, loneliness. What is one to do with loneliness? It creeps into the soul of many a person and it leads them to desperation. Coping with loneliness is an art, and not an art that many can master. You need to be engrossed in "the game of life" in order to escape it. It creeps on me and it creeps on you but most of all it creeps on those whose games are have long intervals.

As a result, Elena started contemplating visiting Paul in prison.

George was not too happy about the visit but could not dissuade her.

"Elena," he said "you are free and have the opportunity to escape your bondage with Paul."

"I know but what am I to do? I haven't been able to find a friend and this loneliness is driving me beserk. Maybe this is my fate and I should be resigned to it."

"Well, I have advised you and that's all I can do. I hope you realize the consequences. It will be worse than before as you are going back to him after all that's happened."

So, Elena took one morning off to visit Paul in prison. Ironically, he was not too displeased to see her.

"So, what brings you here? I am very upset with you for calling the police. We could have settled this between ourselves. I still have 73 days left in this hole."

Elena lifted the fringe of hair from her forehead baring the scars from the stiches.

"Have a look. See what you have done to me instead of ranting and raving like a maniac."

"I'm sure you could have the scars removed."

"With what money? The money you give me each week? The surgeons want $2,000 and I can't borrow it from anyone."

"Stop shouting at me. Cool it. We'll work something out once I get out of this hole you put me in."

"Maybe we should wait for your fictitious grandmother to die and leave you her fortunes."

"Don't disrespect my grandmother."

"How can I? She doesn't even exist. It's a joke. All these years we are waiting for her to die as she is supposed to be very ill. It's funny that I don't know anything about her. For instance, where the hell does she live? Why don't you take me to visit her?"

Elena kept visiting Paul in prison and, sure enough, when his prison term was over, she took him back.

Years passed and life continued as before. Nothing changed. Elena still worked with George and in the restaurant on the weekends. Paul's grandmother never died, if she existed at all, and Paul did not mention her that often any more.

V

One Saturday Elena and Carol decided to spend the whole day together. They would have breakfast together and then go shopping for the rest of the day. But, most important, Elena wanted to discuss her life with her only girlfriend, Carol.

"So, how are you and Paul getting along?"

"You already know the answer. Nothing has changed and I believe nothing will ever change."

"I told you to get rid of the bastard and you had the chance when he was in prison."

"He came back begging. Actually, I found him sitting by the door to the apartments when I came home from work."

"So? Tough luck for him."

"And what about me? I'm all alone. I'm so knocked out all the time that I don't even have the energy to socialize. Anyway, where would I go?"

"You could go to a pub. You'll meet plenty of people there."

"I don't like the type of people who come to the pub."

"I don't know what the hell to tell you. You seem resigned to your life."

"That's my destiny and I am compelled to fulfil it."

"Don't talk rubbish. Your destiny is in your own god-damn hands. It's what you make of it."

"Perhaps it's the destiny of all humanity."

"What do you mean? What are you talking about?"

"I wish the creator, if there is one, would have given me a better role on earth. Perhaps, I could have walked into a cancer ward and cured everyone."

"So you could be rich and powerful and bask in your own glory?"

"I suppose you are right. But it seems that I'm endlessly struggling. And what for?"

"You are not the only one struggling, darling. We all have to strive for a better life."

"You, me, we. All of humanity is struggling, although the better-offs are in a disguised struggle."

"Disguised what?"

"Like pouring spices on food to make it tasty and more palpable."

"So what's the solution?"

"There is no solution In the face of adversity and natural disasters and even worse, in the face of ensuing nothingness, humanity has to huddle like the penguins in the arctic. That's the only way to survive while on this planet."

"Elena, Elena, get hold of yourself. You are on the verge of losing it. Penguins and all."

TO TAHEREH SAFFARZADEH: IN MEMORIUM

It was the summer of 1978 when my wife and I decided to go on a holiday,

We were living in Tehran in a two bedroomed flat with my son who was then six months old and we felt that we really needed a break and especially I needed a pause from my job of teaching literature at the National University of Iran.

My parents, who also lived in a flat, were not far from us and they agreed to look after our son, provided we would not be gone for longer than a month.

We figured that that the best place to go was Tel Aviv as the climate was ideal, sunny and around 30 degrees. We also had a lot of relatives there and could stay with one of my cousins.

When we left, the political climate was calm and quiet, although there were rumours of minor protests against the government in one or two provinces, which generally, the public seemed to ignore.

Two weeks of our holiday had passed and we heard that the protests were now escalating into riots. Indeed, the political climate seemed to be getting murkier and murkier.

I called my parents and demanded that they join us and when calm and quiet would again be restored, we would all return. I had to be back in September as the new semester would be starting and in any case, we were almost penniless.

I called my mother with instructions on what to do.

"Bring what jewellery you can so we can sell them if needs be," I urged.

"I will try to, but what if they confiscate them at the airport?"

"That's a chance that we will have to take." I didn't want to elaborate any more on the phone.

"What about our flats and their contents?" she sobbed.

"Just lock them up and give the keys to the respective neighbours. Tell them you'll be back soon. It's only temporary, till we return."

"I'll call you when I have booked the flights."

Actually, my mother did well. She managed £5,000 and her jewellery.

But peace and calm were not to be restored. Riots and demonstrations continued and turned violent. The shah left the country and the government was overthrown.

We had no choice but to stay in my cousin's flat in Tel Aviv in which he gave us one room and the hallway. My parents stayed in the room in a double bed and my wife and I slept in the hallway together with my son.

My cousin looked after us as best as he could as he himself was on a meagre income. He started early in the morning with his taxi in order to get more spending income. I offered him some money but he refused.

"Keep your money he said. You will need every penny as, at present, your future is uncertain.

"But how will I ever repay you?"

"Don't speak nonsense. Aren't you ashamed of yourself? Shall I charge my relatives rent?"

But we couldn't stay in Tel Aviv forever in our situation, so we decided to go to London where, at least, we would have more access to Tehran and what was going on.

On the way out, I met a friend of mine in the airport, also from Iran, and I followed him as we approached the Israeli security counter. My friend asked the security supervisor not to stamp his passport as he was intending to return to Iran. She complied. I also made the same request but the supervisor stamped my passport. When I asked her why she had intentionally stamped my passport, she replied that I had leant over the counter to make sure and this had annoyed her.

"You have not stamped my friend's passport and I also asked you not to stamp mine. You even nodded in agreement," I whispered.

"You offended me by bending over the counter," she replied curtly.

"And is that a reason to jeopardise my life?"

"Proceed," she replied harshly.

From Heathrow, I called a friend whom I had known for many years and who was working in a hardware shop to ask about accommodation and he gave me the addresses of a few house owners who rented rooms in their houses.

Two months passed and it was now Feb 1978. Our savings were now almost depleted, so I decided to call one of my colleagues to ask about the situation and whether there was a possibility of returning. I had shared an office with Tahereh for many years, so I decided to call her.

"What a surprise, Robert. I was wondering where you were and when I would hear from you."

"I am in London with my wife and son. How is the situation now? Have classes commenced?"

"As a matter of fact, everything has gone back to normal. The registrar is looking for you as the students registered for your classes are awaiting your return. The semester began a week ago."

"Tahereh, I am ready to return but I have some serious concerns about which I need to ask you."

"Firstly, there is the question of my being Jewish. Do you notice any antisemtic sentiments within the community or among the students?"

"Robert dear, if there was, I would be the first to tell you not to return. The students are anxiously waiting for you and you must return by the end of next week. However, there is something that you must do as a precaution."

"What must I do?"

"As the term has already begun and you are not here, you will have to give a reason for your absence and you will have to support it with evidence. Just to be on the safe side. The best excuse I can think of, is a medical excuse. Consult with some doctors and find a discomfort or malady for which you had gone for treatment and from which you have recuperated. That's all I can say."

"Understood. I will call you again shortly."

I asked my friend to help me and he made an appointment with his GP so we could discuss the problem in view of the fact that there was now no time left if I were to return the following week.

The GP could not come up with any ailment that was curable within weeks, especially since it required medical documentation.

"Let us try duodenal ulcers," he suggested. "I can provide you with x-rays of one of my patients in the hope that the authorities will not investigate."

"I will have to take my chances," I replied.

I called Tahereh and informed her that I would be arriving by the end of the week and would meet her Sunday morning in the office.

As I arrived on the campus building, I noticed drastic changes. Groups of students were assembled in the hallways discussing and debating outside their classrooms.

The atmosphere seemed to me to be gloomy and murky. A sombre mood seemed to be prevailing and I noticed black colour to be predominant.

Most female students were wearing black chadors or cloaks which they grasped from within so as not to expose their hands. How would they be able to take notes unless they wear gloves, I wondered. The less religious ones, which were few indeed, wore scarfs which totally covered their heads, including the lower parts of the faces.

I immediately proceeded to my office, where I found Tahereh. She informed me of the courses I had to teach and handed me a schedule.

"Go to room 104, she said. The students are already in the classroom, waiting for you."

I hastened to the class. At the door, I noticed two revolutionary guards shouldering Kalashnikovs and talking to each other in whispers. I decided that the best bet was to ignore them and enter the classroom.

As I was about to enter, their conversation became more audible, most probably intentionally, so as to make me aware:

"Robert Blum is a Zionist," I heard one guard tell the other emphatically.

"We will deal with him after the lecture," replied the other in a subdued tone which was still audible.

I have no idea what and how I lectured that hour. All that kept going through my mind was what fate would await me when I left the classroom.

Perhaps they would ask me to step outside the building and stand against some wall. Then they would proceed to shoot me dead, after which they would visit my wife and the following conversation would probably transpire:

"We have had no choice but to kill your husband. We have found him to be a Zionist. Indeed his passport bears the stamps of entry and exit from the State of Israel."

My wife would probably not answer. She would probably be overwhelmed with grief and maybe crying.

The second guard would presumably continue:

"Should you want his body back, since we know that in the Jewish faith the body has to be interred immediately, we will be happy to bring it to you provided you pay for the bullets used. We each shot him once in an effort not to waste bullets and also to save you expenses."

Probably, the first guard would resume:

"We are extremely sorry, but these are the regulations and we must follow procedures. Two bullets at 250 dollars each, will amount to 500 dollars. We assume that you would not have the money now but will give you 24 hours to provide it. We will be at your door at 8 am tomorrow to collect and should you be in a position to make payment, then you will have the body the folowing morning."

With the lecture over, I sprinted to my office.

Tahereh was seated behind her desk, and as usual, she was surrounded by students seeking advice on various things. I sat at my desk which faced hers and waited for her to be free.

In the many years that I had known Tahereh, I had never seen her to be emotional or excited. She was always calm, focused and serene, no matter what. And, she was always accommodating to the students, staff or other faculty members.

The students having left the room, she turned her gaze towards me and calmly said, "Robert, you owe me your life."

"What," I only managed to utter as I was still in a daze.

"Two revolutionary guards came to the office to wait for you to come back after your class. They said that they wanted to question you and having talked with them in considerable length, I found out what their real intent was and assured them that, having known you these many years, you were basically harmless and I would take any consequential responsibility. So, basically, I informed them that anyone harming you will have to answer to me.

Tahereh had become one of the voices of the revolution but in a literary manner. She was called upon for humanitarian advice from the "authorities" and her poetry was recited on the radio.

Prior to the revolution, Tahereh had been suspended from the university. Even her backpay of six months had been withheld.

It seemed that the secret service of the Shah had decided that her published poetry was not in keeping with their version of democracy. I recall one day when Tahereh graciously read me one of her poems. Naturally, it was in Persian but the content was quite clear, even to me with my limited knowledge of the language.

It voiced the sadness of the fact that there was no safety in the posted letter. At random, it could be opened and scrutinized by the authorities. Naturally, the area from which it was posted would make a big difference as the authorities were aware of the residences and offices of the dissidents.

I didn't know the whys and the wherefores but had heard that they had taken her for interrogation and had threatened her with severe consequences, pointing a gun to her head.

As a result, she was living in a one bedroom apartment in the city with little and possibly no visitors. This I know, as one day the registrar walked down the faculty corridor, knocking on each door with the question, "I have a cheque for Tahereh. Will one of you take it to her?" Silence meant no. No one volunteered to take the cheque for fear of how the Secret Service would deal with them.

I ventured to take the risk. I did not owe it to her to accept the task but, having spent years as her officemate, and knowing how moral and righteous she was, I felt that it was the least I could do for her. I ignored the warnings that my parents gave me regarding the consequences of undertaking such a task and my father's foreboding remark rang in my ears, "son, this may be the last time we might be seeing you."

"Dad, I have to do this if I have any principles or humanity within me."

"But you also have a family and your obligations to them is the priority. Who is going to look after your wife and son should you disappear. I am old and retired and your mother has also aged."

"I still feel that I have to take the chance. However, I believe there is something small in my favour."

"I wonder what that could be."

"It's the fact that we are Jewish. As you know, Jewish people are not targeted where politics are in play as the officials are well aware that they in no way get involved."

"Well, if you have already made up your mind and are adamant, there remains nothing further for me to say. I hope and pray that we will see you soon."

With that, I bade my parents and wife farewell and told them that I hoped that I would return after a few hours.

Perhaps, I should pause here to say something else about Tahereh. Somehow, Tahereh had the ability to envision future occurrences or events which rather reminded me of Nostradamus. One morning as we sat opposite each other in the office, she fixated her eyes unto mine for a few seconds and said:

"Robert, you are going to have a terrible car accident soon."

"Nonsense. This is a figment of your imagination. Are you trying to scare me or something? Since when have you become a prophet?"

"I can feel it," was her calm response. "Your car will be crushed like an accordion but you will escape unhurt."

Nothing further was said on the subject and I dismissed her prediction and forgot about it.

Months passed. One day, I was teaching an evening class when a colleague asked me for a ride home and I naturally agreed.

As I drove, we were busy conversing. We had to cross a highway and I didn't realise that a van was speeding towards us.

My car became a total wreck. As a matter of fact, it had to be towed away the next morning but neither of us was hurt. Tahereh's words were, "your car will crumble like the folding of an accordion." From that day on, I would keep a frightful reverence as to her insights of the future.

So, I went out to find the necessities required by her: soap, coffee, tea, rice, cooking oil and whatever else I could find which I thought she would need. The grocery shops were charging ridiculous prices but it didn't matter. Furthermore, there were long queues and shortages but everything could be found for a price, if not in the stores, then on the black market.

In any case, now things went back to normal and the classes resumed. However, I realized that I was to be under constant tension and stress which was quite unbearable but understandable.

For example, I would get an ex-student whom I had failed, coming to my office to settle his grievances. He no longer pursued his academic career but was now given the role of "defender of the realm." With his machinegun swung over his shoulder he came to see me one morning.

"You do remember me, don't you," he scoffed.

"Of course I do," I responded meekly.

"Your having failed me has changed the whole course of my life. Now I am in the military."

"Look, I didn't fail you. You failed yourself. There has to be a system of right and wrong. Were I to pass you, it wouldn't be fair to the better achievers."

I tried to be as elementary in my conversation as possible. I had to make him understand as well as placate him. He continued, threateningly:

"You know, yesterday we tried to save bullets. We lined up the offenders back to back, shoulder to shoulder, and shot them. We wanted to know how many bodies one bullet would penetrate."

I wasn't sure what else I could say to pacify him. Was he just trying to instil fear or was he actually threatening? Fortunately, at our faculty we always kept our office doors ajar as a welcome sign to the students even when we had confidential situations. This was of some comfort to me in the predicament I was in.

Luckily, at that minute I heard Tahereh walking down the corridor and as always pursued by students, greeting various people on her way to the office. I guess the student confronting me as she entered must have realized his limitations and her authority and facing her, he nodded slightly and exited.

The semester nearing its end, my wife and I decided that it was a good time to leave, and reconsider our options with the view of the situation I was in.

However, this was to be a long, complicated, and tedious process.

While the normal citizens were free to enter and exit the country, there were restrictions on university professors, among other governmental employees. As my official title was that of "assistant professor," I was among those who had to adhere to a series of formal regulations and procedures in order to go for the vacational leave I was applying for.

First of all, I had to have the written consent of the Faculty of Humanities but that posed no problem as I was known and respected by most members.

Secondly, I had to have the permission of the campus "Student's Assembly" which consisted of students from the freshman to the senior years together with a mingling of student revolutionary guards.

Thirdly, the documentation of the first two stages had to be taken to the University Committee, and if endorsed by them, the final stage would be the chancellor's approval and certification.

Tahereh diligently drafted and compiled all the letters for the various departments and after a few weeks consent was granted by all.

The final stage was for me to personally take the endorsed letters to the chancellor for his final decision.

With all the required paperwork in hand, I proceeded to the chancellor's office.

It was about lunchtime and I was quite anxious to finalize everything. The chancellor's office door was locked and the janitor informed me that the chancellor had gone to lunch and after that he would always go for prayers. I would be better off going back to our building and returning in a couple of hours. The chancellor, I presumed, was anxious to portray himself as a devout commoner.

I returned after two hours but the chancellor was still not there. Finally, an old man came and unlocked the door and entered.

He can't possibly be the chancellor, I thought to myself. He was a short, stocky, and balding man, probably in his late sixties. He wore a light brown suit, without a tie as was now the custom, and his shirt collar was worn out. In addition, there were food stains or oil stains on both his lapels. I assumed that he was going in to give the office a final clean before the arrival of the chancellor.

I knocked on the door and since there was no response, I opened the door wide enough to put my head through.

"Can you please let me know when the chancellor will be in?" I queried.

"Come in if you have any business with me," he replied.

He walked down and sat behind his desk.

"I am an assistant professor in the Faculty of Humanities," I began, and I am intending to go abroad in the coming summer holidays. I have brought all the relevant documents for you to look at."

"Hand them to me," he said sneeringly. He didn't even ask me to sit down so I took a couple of steps back from his desk as a matter of courtesy and waited.

"You want to go on a summer holiday," he mimicked me scornfully. "You just came back from a prolonged holiday last summer and you want to go again?"

"With your approval," I answered almost inaudibly.

"You have been the cause of a brain drain from this country. Now many professors want to leave, supposedly for a vacation, and God knows how many will return."

He jotted down a few lines on the letter addressed to him and motioned me to take it. I thanked him for his kindness, took the papers and exited his office. Words cannot tell how exhilarated I was. As I could not read Persian, I assumed that he had scribbled his consent and I dashed back to our faculty as fast as my legs could carry me.

Tahereh remained in the office, in anticipation of the good news.

"I've got the approval," I remarked excitedly.

"Let me read it."

I handed her the papers and waited.

"O my God," she exclaimed.

"What's the matter?"

"The chancellor has written that your request has been denied. You are to write a declaration stating that you are ready at once to serve the revolution and your country and to resume teaching any subject assigned to you."

I was speechless and started panicking.

"Don't worry. I'll draft a letter right away and get it ready for you to sign and hand to the registrar."

In September, after the summer holidays, the courses resumed and I taught the courses I was scheduled to teach.

Then one day, I got a surprise visit from the registrar whom I had gotten to know well enough during the past two years. On occasion, I would visit him in his office and have a chat with him.

"Close the door so we can speak confidentially," he said.

"Is there a problem? You didn't even inform me that you were coming to see me."

"No problem," he replied. "I am aware that you wanted to go on a holiday last summer and your request was denied by the chancellor."

"I did bring my declaration to resume teaching to your office, if you remember."

"Well, would you like to go on a holiday, THIS SUMMER?"

"Yes, of course, but I stand no chance."

"I can help you but prior to giving you any information, I need to ask you for a favour."

"What kind of favour?"

"My daughter needs some medication which is not available here. Would you be able to find it and mail it to me? I presume that you are going to England but I believe that you can find it in any European country."

"Don't be silly. Of course, I will and with pleasure. I would do it even without your intention of helping me, if I can."

"Okay, let's go on. As you are aware it's illegal to own properties or have bank accounts abroad."

"Yes, I know."

"Well, the chancellor owns a beautiful house in Brighton and his wife and two daughters live there." He paused, putting his thoughts together. "I suggest that you go through the various stages of your application as you have done before and bring these facts up in the course of your conversation when you approach the chancellor again. He is not that lowly, devout commoner which he portrays himself to be. He is not even a good actor."

Prior to the summer holidays, I managed to go through the whole ordeal again. However, the procedure was easier as the stages had already been traversed and all that was necessary was for each department to renew the consent by resigning and dating the original applications. This the registrar provided.

"You again,?" the chancellor resounded emphatically when I saw him for the second time. "I thought, I made my position clear to you in our last meeting."

"By the way, sir," I replied slyly. "I have heard that your daughters are doing well in their school in Brighton. And what a majestic house they live in!"

A word to the wise is sufficient. The chancellor was stunned and stupefied. He signed the letter and motioned me to come forward and pick it up. He only uttered one word, "leave."

Years later, Tahereh called me from the Iranian Embassy in London where I met her and her husband. She asked me

whether I would consider returning to teach but she knew well
enough that that was impractical.

I have always treasured Tahereh's friendship and I will cherish
her memory forever.

ELIAS

He walked into my electrical shop, rested his two elbows on my counter and looked me in the eyes.

A few paces behind him, right by the entrance to the shop, stood my father-in-law, George.

My father-in-law had told me about his friend Elias who needed a job just to keep busy. "If you don't work, you die," he said "and Elias would rather be interrupted by the devil rather than wait for him."

"But he is too old to be of any use," I had remarked. "He is almost 75. What could he do in an electrical shop?"

"He is not asking for any money. He only wants to be occupied. Just keep him busy. Let him make you and your staff coffee and sandwiches, perhaps tidy the shop or any other thing you may think of. Should you wish to give him a few pounds at the end of each week, that would be decent of you. If not, Elias will not be complaining."

George had a tendency of rambling on and on. He would intersperce his words with sayings, proverbs, and hearsay and he was not about to let me off without them this time either.

And so, he continued, "you know, there is a giving hand and a taking hand. Few people are blessed with the giving hand. Everyone knows the story of the man who fell in the well. All the villagers gathered round the well and asked the man to 'give' them his hand. But the man refused. As it happened, his friend passed by and the villagers ran to him to inform him of the situation. His friend said that he would pull the man out of the well at once. He went to the well and called to his friend to 'take' his hand and his friend responded immediately and was out of the well."

I had no choice in the matter. I had to oblige my father-in-law. So I asked Elias to return at 8 am the following Monday.

My father-in-law approached Elias, put his arm round his shoulder and they both walked out of the shop.

On Monday morning when I arrived at 7:45 am, I found Elias standing by the door. "You're early," I said but he didn't reply. He waited for me to lift the shutters and unlock the door. He then proceeded directly to the kitchen to make me a cup of coffee. He didn't even ask me whether I wanted tea or coffee. I found out that my coffee had milk in it and was awfully sweet but I didn't say anything.

In fact, Elias didn't say anything much all day. He positioned himself in the corner of the entrance to the shop and would stay there all day looking at the activity in the street. He would only move away when he had to go to the loo or when he felt that he had to make us sandwiches or coffee. He would never ask us anything and one would think that he was dumb. He would bring us what he wanted. After serving us, he would resume his position by the entrance. On some occasions when I had to serve customers and bring them some goods, he would leave his space and follow me to the shelves and say "give it to me to carry." If the item was not heavy, I would hand it to him, making him feel useful.

Elias never talked much. He would nod when you greeted him in the morning and grunt, which meant goodby, when he left in the afternoons. Some serious thing must have happened to him in the past but he was not about to open up to me. I knew that I had to give him time to open up, so I started by asking him petty questions about himself and his family. Elias would always give the tersest of answers in a subdued voice, making me aware that his replies were being forced out of him. Sorrow had imbedded itself in his voice and in the wrinkles on his face. Any attempt to force him out of shell on my part would only cause him to suffer further. So, I left him to himself with as little communication as possible in the hope that someday he would divulge his past of his own accord.

Then one day, an incident occurred that somewhat jerked Elias out of his shell. Elias had been occupying his usual corner by the door when I heard him scream, "Ricky, Ricky, come quickly."

I dashed towards the entrance, "what's the matter?"

"Two men with balaclavas have just come out of the Bank of Barroda next door."

"They have just passed the shop! Come see, come see! They are not even running, just walking. Now they are removing their balaclavas. Shall I follow them?"

I rushed to the door. "Don't even look at them. Quickly come inside, you stupid fool. Have you the legs or the strength to follow them?"

Somehow the incident proved to be the catalyst to his opening up to me.

Then one day, when business was quiet, I approached him and asked him to make me a cup of coffee. "Please don't put any sugar or milk," I said.

"Why don't you talk to me and let me help you, that is, if I can. It's not good to keep everything pent up inside yourself."

"I am beyond help. My life is not worth anything."

"But you have a wife and children. What about them? Are you not responsible for what becomes of them? Or, don't you care?"

"Of course I care. If it wasn't for them, I would most probably kill myself. But there is no way I can help them. What could I do for them? I'm too old and useless. Nothing matters to me anymore."

"Don't talk nonsense. Don't you think that just being around them helps? I had a friend who didn't like his wife but he seldom left the house. I asked him why he didn't go out more often? They lived in separate rooms within the house and didn't communicate much. 'Is it because you don't want to spend money,' I asked? 'No', he replied, 'the fact that she knows that there is someone in the house gives her a sense of comfort.' "Do you understand me Elias?"

"I suppose that you are right," Elias answered reluctantly. "You are not aware of my problems, so it's easy for you to justify everything."

He continued with a subdued tone of voice, "We live in a council flat not far from the shop. My wife basically does the house chores. My daughter, who is now 35 years old and still single, does any cleaning job she can get and is only busy on the average of twice a week, if that. My son, who is almost 40, is employed in a bakery three times a week. In short, we struggle to survive."

"Tell me about your past. You seem to be very good friends with my father-in-law."

Elias remained silent for a minute or so. A deep sigh emerged from the depths of his rue laden heart. He lowered his head so as not to meet my gaze and he continued......

"My sister and I were born in Baghdad. We were middle class citizens and my father had a small carpentry shop in the city. He sold doors and small items of furniture like little chairs and tables. He also sold accessories such as locks, handles and hinges. People would also bring furniture that needed to be repaired or upholstered. You cannot say that we were very well-off, but we made a decent living. I suppose you could have classified us being in the lower middle classes."

"Everyone knew that we were Jewish but this didn't bother us in the least and we felt that we were liked by the community. In fact, most of our clients were Muslims. I myself believe that it is politics and governments that cause discriminations and prejudices."

"We left Baghdad in 1944. The air was getting polluted with anti-semitic feelings and my father thought it would be best to pack up and go to Iran. So, we sold our shop and left."

I didn't want to interrupt him now that he was in a talkative mood. I waited for him to catch his breath.

"I was fifteen years old and my sister was twelve when we arrived in Tehran. We stayed with friends for about two months during which time my father found a shop in the outskirts of the city. He started by selling electrical appliances like small fridges, radios, and tv's and also renting them out."

"Life was pleasant under the Shah. As was the case in Iraq, our neighbours, both at home and in the business knew that we were Jewish but we were never discriminated against and felt very much part of the community."

"How big was the Jewish community in Tehran?" I asked. I had so many questions that I wanted to ask but did not for fear of his losing his stream of thoughts.

I believe that in the whole of Iran there must have been fourty to fifty thousand. They were scattered in the provinces and many had changed their names to Muslim ones in fear of persecution."

"In any case, my sister got married to a Muslim and she disappeared. I don't know where in hell they went but we never heard from them again. I too got married to my first cousin who had also come from Iraq. My friends warned me about marrying a close relative. They insisted that this was medically wrong and that, under Jewish rules, one could only marry a third generation cousin. But, in short, I did not have the temperament or strength of character to look for someone. I suppose it was a matter of convenience."

I could see the tears swelling in his eyes but decided to keep silent.

"I started noticing that perhaps my children were not as bright as my wife and I. Deep down, I knew the reason but I kept supressing the truth. It would break my heart watching them play with other children. Of course, the small playmates didn't notice anything but my fear was of the future."

Elias stopped a moment to catch his breath and wipe the tears.

"Then I started rationalizing to shroud my guilt. I was relatively new to the community, I told myself. How was I to find a wife? Firstly, I would have had to prove myself a successful businessman and then I would have had to go through the whole process of courtship and to be scrutinized by the girl's family."

"On the other hand, there was my cousin Margaret. She was always in our house with her parents. Her mother kept nagging Margaret and telling her that she was getting old. Soon she would be an old maid as she was nearing 30. And there I was, ready to be harnessed."

Two electricians walked in and stood at the counter, so Elias went silent and walked to the rear of the shop towards the kitchen.

Days passed and months passed but Elias remained silent. He would avoid eye contact with me and would move away when I approached him. He preferred to be left alone and I learned to respect that. I noticed that Elias had a protruding stomach above his belt and I wondered why, as besides a single sandwich and a couple of coffees, he ate nothing at all.

One morning as I was parking my car across the road from the shop, I noticed that Elias was not waiting outside the shop as usual. That seemed odd as he was never late throughout the months. As the morning progressed, I started to worry, especially since Elias had no phone and there was no way for me to contact him.

Elias did not show up that day and the only person who would know where he lived was my father- in-law. Unfortunately, he did not have a phone either.

The following morning I went to the shop at 7:30. I opened the shop and stood behind the counter, looking out into the street. Sure enough Elias arrived at 7:45. He was walking slowly, dragging his feet. Agony was resident in his face. He walked in, rested his two elbows on the counter across from me and whispered, "can we talk?"

"Of course," I answered reassuredly. "Come in. I'll lock the door and we'll go down to the basement." I led the way, flicking the switch at the top of the stairs, and he climbed down step by step clutching on to the railings.

We sat on two chairs in the basement, facing each other.

"What's the problem Elias? Why didn't you call me on Monday?"

"I had this agonizing pain in my stomach all morning. It seemed as if my whole stomach was on fire. I called the ambulance and they took me to the emergency section of the hospital. I waited all afternoon before a doctor came to see me and told me that I need an MRI. He told me that it could be cancer. You know that my wife died of cancer two years ago and she suffered terribly."

"Let's not jump to conclusions. It could be a passing pain, maybe indigestion from something you ate that caused you acidity."

"In any case, I have to go for the MRI on Friday."

"Do you want me to come with you?"

"No, I can manage. Besides, your father-in-law insists on coming." He hesitated, not knowing how to put the words together. "I have £20,000 that I want you to keep for me till I undergo the tests. It's my life savings."

"That's a big responsibility. For arguments' sake, suppose, God forbid, that something were to happen to you. Your children could come to me and claim the amount of £100,000 instead of £20,000. I'm sure they know about the money. What would I do then?"

Elias didn't know what to answer. I reflected a moment and continued, "I suppose we can get two friends to witness and sign everything. Do you mind?"

"You are doing me a big favour," he mumbled.

"Let me know when you want to bring the money so I can make the necessary arrangments."

"It's here with me."

Elias stood up, took off his coat, lowered his trousers, and unbuttoned the lower part of his shirt. Tied around his waist were three packs of fifty pound notes bundled in a white tablecloth. He had used safety pins pinned to his shirt to stop the package from falling. The protrusion round his belly, which I had noticed before, now disappeared.

"I'll hide this wrapper in the basement for today till I get two friends to witness everything tomorrow. Somehow I'll have to stop the staff from going down to the basement."

"That's okay with me. As I have no choice, I'll have to take my chances."

Elias had the MRI done on Friday and came to the shop the following Monday with the results in his pocket. He was out of breath as he waited for me to read the results.

"Elias, you should take the results to your GP," I said.

"I need to know now," he managed.

I took the letter out of the envelope and skimmed it, finding the words "gastric ulcer".

"Elias, you don't have any type of "cancer". You have a stomach ulcer and I'm sure your doctor will give you the proper medication."

Embarassment coupled with relief lit up his face. The saying "a little knowledge is a dangerous thing" came to my mind. Elias kept coming to the shop for the next few months and I eagerly awaited the catalyst that would open him up for the rest of his story.

CHAPTER II

Time fades everyday memories but memories of sufferings are deeply etched in the brain forever. Elias' countenance attested to such memories which would remain his partner for the rest of his life.

It took more than a year for Elias to bring himself to utterly confide in me and to reveal to me his story.

Elias had owned a shop in Tehran renting and selling radios, televisions and other electronic accessories. One of his clients was the American Embassy and this came to the attention of the Revolutionary Guards.

One morning, Elias couldn't remember the date or the month, four Revolutionary Guards dressed in black from head to toe and carrying Kalashnikovs on their shoulders pushed open the door and rushed to the back of the shop where Elias was sitting behind his counter.

"Is your name "Elias?" demanded one of the guards who seemed to be the leader.

"Yes," muttered Elias not knowing what to expect. He rose to his feet as a sign of showing them respect.

"You are a son of a bitching traitor," continued the leader in a threatening tone. "We have invoices of TV's that you have rented to our enemy, the American Embassy. What have you got to say about this?"

One of the other guards produced some papers which he waved at Elias' face.

"I'm just a businessman," Elias responded in an apologetic tone. He lowered his head so as not to look any of them in the eyes, so as not to appear confrontational. "I didn't know that it was illegal to rent TV's to the American Embassy."

"Let me take care of him boss," shouted one of the subordinate guards, clenching his fist and punching Elias in the face.

Elias reeled and fell unto his chair which toppled to the ground. His nose was broken and was bleeding profusely. Another guard produced a cable tie and tied Elias' hands behind his back.

The leader added, "these Zionist pigs must learn a lesson."

While Elias still lay on the floor bleeding and un-conscious, all four started emptying the contents of the shop and placing them in the back of their van. The radios and Tv's that were too old to be of any value were smashed with the butt of their rifles. That done, they lifted Elias and placed him on top of their haul.

When Elias came to, he was lying on his back. He could hear the voices of people whispering all around him. Some were kneeling and trying to soothingly talk to him. As his vision cleared, he could see the frame of a metal mesh above him.

Was he in a cage? "Indeed you are," said one of his cellmates in a hushed voice. "We are all in a cage, twenty of us and we reckon that we are twenty miles to the east of the capital."

Cleaning the blood on his face, they helped him to his feet and told him to be careful when touching his face as his nose was broken and could bleed again.

Conscious again, Elias could see rows of cages both behind and in front of his cage. Each cage was about 25 square meters and contained roughly about 20 prisoners. There were rows of cages as far as the eye could see.

Guards would bring them food and water once a day and they would have to learn to share amicably. Otherwise there would be consequences. A deep hole had been dug on the corner of each cell to serve as a toilet. There were no sanitaries. Each prisoner was brought in with the clothes he was wearing at the time of his arrest and they were all living in the open and were at Nature's mercy. Fortunately for Elias, he was arrested in the summer and the weather was fairly warm.

Two guards, carrying rifles, batons, and cuffs patrolled each row of cages.

At irregular times, two special guards would come to take away a prisoner for questioning and punishment, if they deemed it necessary. Rarely would a prisoner return unscathed. All who returned, and some did not, were beaten, whipped, and bloodied but none would ever disclose his ordeal.

Months passed and the weather was getting colder. Soon winter would be upon them and the prisoners wondered whether they would be relocated to more insulated prisons or whether they would be the casualty of the elements.

Then, one morning they came for him.

"Are you sick and tired of this cage, old man?" said one of the guards sarcasticallyl "We are moving you to more pleasant and comfortable accomodations."

They handcuffed Elias, blindfolded him and walked him to the van. The journey must have taken an hour or so but Elias wasn't sure. When he climbed down from the van, he felt that he was walking on sand and stones. Then he climbed some steps up and then some steps down.

When the captors removed his blindfold, he found himself in a cave, a cave that might have been dug on the side of some hill. It was dark inside and the only light that came in was from the metal door through which they had entered. The hole, for you cannot call this a cave, must have had about five meters of space, although it was neither square or round. It must have been dug irregularly to hold one person captive. The height of the roof must have been about seven feet as Elias was 5'8" tall.

The guards said nothing. They just closed and locked the door and Elias was left in total darkness. Fortunately, a tiny ray of light intruded the cave from the gap to the hinges. Elias crouched to one corner of the cave but feeling that it would be warmer and more comfortable towards the entrance, he sat and leaned his back to the entrance. Hours passed but he could not tell how many. It must have been night time when he heard footsteps and moved away from the door. The door was opened and one of the guards left a tray inside. Elias found out that the food consisted as some kind of thick soup together with a slice of bread and a glass of water. The same meal was brought to him twice a day, one around mid-day and one at night.

A couple of months must have passed but Elias couldn't keep track of time anymore. The decision had been made to gradually starve Elias to death by reducing his rations of food and water. At first, the amount of food was slowly cut and Elias slowly realized what they were up to. He was feeling weaker and weaker.

After sometime, there no longer was any food, only two glasses of water, one in the morning and one in the evening. The guard bringing the water said, "Soon you won't even have any water to drink, you fucking bastard. We know how to get rid of traitors like you."

"Why are you trying to starve me to death?" Elias sobbed. "What am I being accused of? Are there no courts or a system of justice?"

Neither of the two guards answered. One of them took two dried prunes from his pocket, gave one to his friend, and put the other in his mouth, chewing the flesh and swallowing it.

"This is instead of your meal," he said, spitting the pit into Elias' face. They then walked out and locked the door.

Elias groped the ground, and having found the pit, cleaned it with his shirt and kept it in his mouth for what seemed to him like a week. There was some sugary taste left which would soon disappear but at least it kept him occupied.

After one week, there was no food and no water. Elias believed that now he had nothing to lose. He had to confront the guards when they would come to check on him. When they did, it luckily happened to be the following Friday and this seemed to be fortunate for Elias in terms of what he had to say.

"Please listen to me a minute for God's sake," Elias muttered.

The two guards hesitated. They had come to check on Elias' condition. "I would like to ask you a small question before you leave me. Like you, I have a wife and two children and you should pity them, if not me. Tell me, didn't your prophet Ali

instruct you not to let anyone to die of thirst? Even in
the street and especially in the bazaar where I used to go, there
are metal containers full of water with a chained cup to quench
the thirst of the passer-by. Are you all disbelievers? Surely, you
will have to answer God for what you are doing to me."

The guards didn't say a word and exited.

The next morning the two guards came for Elias. "Get up"
one of them said. "You have been summoned to court for
sentencing." "We have brought you a glass of water to quench
your thirst and give you energy to speak in court", said the
other, handing Elias a glass of water which he had brought
with him.

Elias was not cuffed or blindfolded. The guards waited for
him to drink the water and walked him to their van, each
supporting him on one shoulder.

Elias could not describe the courthouse but said it consisted of
about two dozen long benches. The front bench was meant for
the accused with a guard to each side. The remaining benches
were for the public, men only. The last few benches were for
the women and children.

The guards escorted Elias to the second bench as another
prisoner's case was being heard on the front bench. He was
wearing a dirty faded blue jean, and a short-sleeved white shirt
which was worn out at the collar. He seemed to be in his late
fifties, short, stocky and bald. In front was the cleric standing
behind a podium with an armed guard on either side.

The cleric ordered the accused man to stand up so that the
charges against him could be read.

"You have been caught red-handed robbing a flat on Shiraz Avenue on September the 1st," began the Cleric. "You were given chase and caught. Do you deny this?"

"No, your honour."

"Obviously. There is nothing to deny. Facts are facts and you are being judged in accordance with your deeds."

"Islam is a merciful religion but there is no place in it for thieves. This is not your first crime as you and I know. You were convicted for several robberies and spent some time in jail but you haven't changed your ways. On this occasion, you were carrying a knife which was confiscated and is on exhibit. Have you got anything to say?"

It became so silent, you could hear a pin drop.

"Then it is the decision of this court that you be returned to your cell to await execution by hanging at dawn. May God have mercy on your soul." The two guards on either side of the prisoner held the prisoner's arm in readiness to take him to his cell.

The court became noisy again with outbursts of emotion and chatterings. Suddenly, a violent, wailing scream erupted from the back benches. It was a young girl who had risen to her feet and was sobbing and screaming at the top of her lungs. The woman next to her was trying to yank her down by pulling down her dress but to no avail.

"Silence," shouted the Cleric. "What is the meaning of this and who are you?"

An eight year old girl with dishevelled hair flowing to her waist and tears rolling down her cheeks was the only one left standing in the court.

"My mother is dead and now you are hanging my father. Who is to take care of me?"

The Cleric turned his head to the prisoner, "Is this your daughter?"

"Yes, your honour."

"Where is her mother?"

"She died in childbirth."

"If this is true, pending further investigations and conditions to be set by the court, you will be released by the court next week."

He motioned to the guards, "take him back to his cell."

It was now Elias' turn and the guards moved him to the first row.

Elias didn't notice an expression or emotion on the Cleric's face.

He looked at Elias, who stood about ten meters away, "We have been studying your case for the past week and find ......" The Cleric paused for about half a minute fumbling in the file in front of him.

"We have been studying your case" repeated the Cleric, "and find that your only crime is that of doing business with the enemy ...." Again, there was a pause. The Cleric continued, "In view of your age and in view of the fact that there are no adverse records against you, we have decided to release you. The goods and monies that have been confiscated will remain our property and your confinement of 167 days are sufficient punishment for your crime. You may go."

CHAPTER III

Elias stayed with me just over a year. During that year his daughter got married and emigrated. He was left with his son and since his son could not hold a steady job and since his own health was failing, he decided he would quit to spend more time with him.

I was sorry to have him leave as I had gotten attached to him. With him around, I felt that there was always someone there. It's difficult to explain what I mean. Not someone to communicate with, but someone whose presence seemed to fill a void.

In any case, one evening my wife gave me a shopping list and asked me to go the High Street. From across the road, I saw an ambulance with flashing lights parked just outside the shops.

They were carrying someone on a stretcher into the ambulance. As they tried to shut the rear door of the ambulance, I heard someone pleading with the medics.

"Please take me to the hospital with him," he wailed.

"We are not allowed to, as he is dead" replied one of the medics.

The ambulance door was shut and it sped away. The siren could be heard in the distance.

Elias' son sat on the pavement, palming his bowed head with both hands.

GABRIELLA

Gabriella, or Gabi, as she was called, sat facing the computer in her office. It was Friday evening, 7:30 PM and all the office staff had long since gone for the weekend. But she was still there.

Where could she go but home? She didn't have a date. Indeed, she hadn't had one for quite a long time, not a serious fellow anyway. She might have had a casual outing for a coffee but nothing one might call a date. Her chances were limited for many reasons. She was not particularly good looking or sexually appealing. She was slender, six foot two inches tall, and flat chested, with short dark brown hair. Sometimes, one feels that if he or she is in the company of others "love grows on you." Unfortunately, she had two male and two female colleagues working with her and they were all married.

So, she only had home to go to, where her mother Cornelia would be waiting as usual. But there was no hurry. She drowned herself in her work to keep monotony at bay.

She had the dual job of receptionist and book-keeper in the lighting-design company she was working for. Two jobs were enrolled into one but she never complained. Leaving the job would immerse her in the harsh realities of life.

Her mother was always nagging her about her social life. She had to go places where she would be in contact with people. Even a library or a supermarket would do. She needn't buy anything but she would have to have the nerve to approach people.

Gabriella knew full well, that by killing time, she was killing life itself. In her mind, she had set a deadline for marriage and childbirth. At the most, she had to be thirty years old when she would deliver the first child. She was now twenty eight and she would need to be pregnant for nine months. This didn't leave her much time.

She had learned that the younger a woman would be while bearing the child, the healthier the child would be. After thirty, the child would be deprived from the many benefits that a mother would be able to give it.

She desperately needed to find someone. She wasn't particularly fussy. Any decent person would do. She would tolerate his being ten years or even fifteen years older than her. He would need to have a job that would ensure a simple life and, above all, he would have to be a practicing Christian.

She would have as many children as God would give her. Children! Children! After all, God had commanded mankind to "go forth and multiply." She had often dreamt of having children and in her mind's eye, she had pictured them at various stages of childhood.

Childbirth was a basic experience to a woman. To be deprived of it would be comparable to a solitary, barren tree, swaying in the autumnal wind of life. Childbirth would be a complete cycle of experience and, although she was no Odysseus, she would do everything in her power not to miss it. Every new sense was an experience. She had seen on TV how a painter would paint the same building hundreds of times in different angles and in different light intensities and in different weather conditions. So, she thought, experience must be as infinite as the universe and one had to taste as much of it as possible.

In the centre of the room where she sat were four desks, positioned two by two, facing each other. Each desk had a telephone and computer on it. To the right of the desks was a door to the room and as you entered, there were five chairs alongside the wall for the guests or messengers the office might have. Across the door, on the other side of the room, was a large window where the boss would sit with his back to it, facing to the side of the four employees.

Gabi occupied the chair in the first row, to the left of her boss. Outside the hall was a room used as a storage together with a kitchenette and a toilet.

Gabi had been in the company for five years now. She was punctual, arriving at eight every morning. While all the employees would leave a five PM, Gabi would linger on. She had the keys and would make sure that she had done everything she could, not leaving anything for the next day.

Her boss Daniel was well aware of Gabi's situation. He felt that he had to pay her extra wages for doing two jobs and staying late almost every day. But he decided that as long as she didn't complain, remained submissive, obeying him without the least of objections, he would let things ride.

In fact, little by little, he started taking liberties. He would call her at odd hours like on a Sunday morning at 9 AM, saying that she had not completed this and that and that she should meet him in the office urgently.

Daniel brooded on a physical relationship with Gabi. After all, he had the place which would cost him nothing and the conditions were perfect. He felt that Gabi would succumb to his advances and would keep the affair to herself. He would buy her some presents and eventually give her a raise.

He pictured it time and again in his mind. He would ask her to work late with him one evening on some project. Around 10 PM, he would start yawning and pretend he was exhausted. "What a rough day I've had. All my bones are aching," he would say. He would then make some kind of physical contact with her, like brushing her arm, which would eventually lead to her massaging his shoulders. He would then put his arms round her neck and draw her towards him. He would then proceed to lightly kiss her on the forehead. Surely, she would respond positively and return the kiss.

He would then sit her on his lap and start to undress her. He pictured her naked, with his right hand stroking her long, slender back and his left hand cupping her tiny breast. Oftentimes, feeling aroused, he would lock the office door and masturbate.

But Daniel had to consider the consequences. Gabi's feelings would not worry him. As far as he was concerned, this would purely be a physical relationship with no emotional attachments. His wife might present a problem. She was quite smart and she had a sixth sense in feminine dimensions. She could smell out the relationship like a cat smelling tuna. He could not jeopardise his family life. He had better leave this relationship with Gabi as a fantasy.

It was happening more and more often. Gabi would look into the computer and would feel dazed. The screen would blur and her whole life would come in front of her. Her mother had named her Gabriella, after the archangel who was the bearer of good tidings. What she needed now was for the trumpeter to awaken her from her dreary life.

Gabi was the only child born to an unwedded couple whose passion had started to fade after marriage.

Gabi's mother, Cornelia, gave birth to her daughter when she was nineteen. At 47, she was a petite woman and, by common standards, a good-looking woman. She was five foot four inches tall, slender, and had dyed her brunette hair blond. Though she could pass as a 35 year old woman, she made no special effort to enhance her appearance.

Cornelia worked part-time as an aide to a dentist. She had had this job for ten years now, with no other interest in life except for her daughter Gabi. She would work from nine to two PM every day, Monday through Friday. On her way home, she would buy some groceries and slowly make her way to the flat. Once home, she would busy herself, tidying the flat, cooking dinner, and, most important of all, waiting for Gabi. Nothing distracted her.

She would move the bed from one corner of the room to the other, complain to herself that the shelves in the living-room needed changing. The kitchen needed redecoration and the circular fluorescent in the kitchen wasn't bright enough. Everybody was using low energy these days, she would mumble. If only she could save some money, she would install six new lights in her 3×3 kitchen.

The kitchen wooden worktop had hairline cracks in it and she wished to change it to grey granite. The washer-dryer looked very old and would sometimes make a rumbling noise. But worst of all was the state of the cutlery and the kitchen utensils. They certainly had to be changed. Suppose Gabi would bring a suitor to the flat! And, finally, the walls and ceilings needed a new coat of paint. All the walls would be magnolia and the ceilings white and that would give the proper contrast.

Besides the kitchen, Cornelia's flat had one bedroom which could hardly hold the double bed which she and her husband had shared. As you entered the flat, the kitchen was directly in front of you. To the left of the entrance hall was the bathroom and across from it was the bedroom. At the end of the corridor, next to the bedroom, was a living room. A sofa stood by the door as you entered the living room with a large window across from it.

From the window of the kitchen or the living room, you could see a block of over a hundred flats rising to ten floors. The façade had become grey from decades of pollution and automobile fumes. Clothes, sheets, and underwear hung from many of the windows and balconies of the occupants.

Sensing that it would soon be home-coming time for Gabi, Cornelia's face brightened up as she busily worked. There was almost no hope of Gabi's friends introducing a man to her, she thought. But a client could walk in. He needn't be wealthy but he had to be Orthodox. Religion brings out the fairer side of man.

She glanced at her watch. It was 8:30 but she was not worried. It was not too late and even if Gabi was to be late, she would never fail to call.

Cornelia was a strong-willed, domineering woman. Her husband, who was five years older than her, finally left her when she was forty.

The saying goes that "mischief often greets an idle man." So Bogdan had stayed in the flat loafing about all day. He had no wish to find a job, not even a part-time one. He would read newspapers or watch TV or just simply do nothing. He was also eating her out of house and home. She complained that there were crumbs everywhere and the loo and bath were dirty. He never cleaned after himself. Above all, he spent his benefits on himself.

His very presence began to irritate her even though he would say nothing at all. One afternoon when she entered the flat and found him eating in bed with a sandwich and beer by his side, she thought that she had had it with him.

"Why don't you find a part-time job instead of being idle all day long for God's sake,?" she screamed. "you could at least become an office cleaner or something and contribute to your family. What about the benefits you receive? We never see a penny of it."

"I'll find a job soon," Bogdan said quietly, hoping to placate her. "You're so sexy when you go bezerk. Come, let's go to bed and I promise everything will be okay. Gabi is not due home for another few hours."

'll never sleep with you, you selfish bastard. I'd rather sleep with the devil."

"Oh, so you're sleeping with your doctor friend, are you?"

She controlled her anger. It was better not to reply, not to say anything. Silence is the best response when confronted with idiocy.

Walls of silence developed between them. Few words were ever exchanged and only the necessary was said. They avoided each other's eyes and there was always tension when they were together in the flat, so much so, that staying under the same roof became unbearable.

Bogdan decided that he must keep away, remain out of sight. The mounting tension had dampened his spirit and would soon destroy him.

Since Cornelia would return from her job at about 2:30 PM every afternoon, he decided to leave the flat at 1:30 every day and stay out as much as possible. Loneliness had become his companion. He would go on long walks and sit on the benches in the park, watching the children play from a distance. There was no one to speak to, but there was such a constant dialogue within himself that sometimes he wouldn't notice the people walking past him. He would walk to the shopping mall to amuse himself but he wouldn't remember how he got there. He was there, as if he were transported by a cloud.

No matter how much he suffered, Bogdan decided not to return home sooner than11 or 12 each evening in the hope that Cornelia would be sleeping. His escapades were wearing him down. He was losing weight and he was always hungry,

One evening he decided to go to one of the local pubs to have a beer and something to eat. He knew that his relationship with Cornelia was fractured beyond repair and she would soon ask him to leave. You have to be resigned to your fate, he thought.

He ordered a ham sandwich and a beer and stood by the bar. It was 10 PM but the pub only had a few people, probably due to the hard times. He looked around. In the corner of the pub there was a woman sitting on her own with a bottle of beer. He kept looking at her direction and she looked back. He couldn't be so lucky, he thought. Perhaps her companion had gone to the toilet.

Half an hour passed but the lady was still alone and throwing glances in his direction. He decided that he would go over and talk to her. What did he have to lose? At the worst, she would tell him to fuck off. Should he ask her for matches? Should he ask her for the time? It didn't matter, It was not an earth-shaking decision. He finally gathered enough courage and asked her if he could sit down.

They spent hours and days meeting each other and, as it turned out, they had much in common.

Irene was also tired of her husband and her life. She needed to escape from home and her only outlet was the pub and alcohol. Her two sons had grown up and had gone their separate ways. Her husband was a pensioner who was spending all his pension on booze and was rarely sober. In short, there was no escape for her until she met Bogdan.

Bogdan met Irene daily, sometimes in the pub but more often in the streets. Together, they planned their getaway. They would go to live in some remote village, away from civilization, and the barest of necessities would suffice them.

One night Bogdan came home so drunk that he could hardly stand on his feet. His head was spinning and he felt the warm surge of vomit forcing its way up his throat. All he needed was to go to bed, lie on his back and cushion his head on top of two pillows to force the vomit down.

Cornelia was in bed but had found it hard to sleep. As soon as she heard the dragging of feet and a key slipping into the lock, she shut her eyes and pretended to be asleep. Bogdan did not turn on the lights but simply staggered to his side of the bed. He was not in any shape to get into his pyjamas. As he was about to lift the covers, Cornelia fidgeted, pretentiously yawned, turned herself to her side facing him and half-opened her eyes.

"Where have you been, you drunken son of a bitch? In the brothels? You stink to high heaven. And what right have you got to wake me up like this every night?"

Bogdan did not answer. He didn't have the strength and it would only fuel the fire.

"I am sick and tired of you. You are worthless as a father, as a husband, and as a breadwinner. You are nothing but scum. How can I go to work in the morning if I don't get any sleep?"

""I am leaving you," Bogdan slurred.

"Go to hell and never return. I want you out of here by the time I come back from work tomorrow. And don't leave anything behind as I don't want to see your face anymore."

Cornelia looked at her watch again: 9:30. She became a little anxious but not worried. Gabi would surely call if her plans were to change. But what about the unexpected? What if there was an accident? I'd better wipe out these thoughts from my mind because if you think of them, they might happen, she thought.

Gabi had become so dependent on her mother that she had lost all self- confidence. She would narrate the minutest details of her daily activities to her mother during dinner and together they would hash and rehash everything. To Gabi, her mother's suggestions and advice were of utmost importance. So much so, that Gabi had become a puppet manipulated by her mother's strings.

Their total income was necessary for them to survive. Mother and daughter had to allocate every cent to basic necessities and it hardly seemed to suffice. Cornelia dreaded to think what would happen if her daughter were to find someone and move out. If nothing else, loneliness would finish her.

She would have to make sure that if Gabi were to find someone, it would satisfy her way of life. He would have to be caring and considerate to his mother-in-law. He would have to live in the vicinity so that they could visit her at least twice a week and would be able to help her should she need it. Although she believed that one's church is in the heart, she would prefer her son-in-law to be a church goer. Religion, she always told her daughter, kept men righteous.

On Saturday evening she might be asked to babysit. Having fed the baby (and later on babies), she would put him or her to sleep and then proceed to clean the house, do the dishes, and maybe iron some clothes. She was overwhelmed with a sense of gratification.

The sound of a key turning in the lever lock whisked her out of her dream.

"Why are you so late? Anything happened?"

"Just the usual. I'm knackered and hungry."

"I cleaned the flat a little and made you some vegetable soup, sausages, and a mixed salad, You have to get some healthy food into your system, simply because you are eating all that rubbish in the office. I also washed your clothes and ironed them. You have two shirts ready, one for Saturday and one for Sunday Church."

Cornelia did not have the nerve to say "Saturday night" since she knew full well that Gabi wouldn't have a date. It was the same story every day, the same sermon.

"Mamma, why are you doing all this? I keep telling you that I'm quite capable of doing it myself."

"What else is left for me to do but to take care of my little child?"

"How many times have we talked about this? Try to go out with some of your friends. Maybe, you'll meet someone. You need a companion, someone to share your life now that your husband is gone. You're still young and pretty. What if I, myself, meet someone?"

"You are my life. Without you, my life would end."

Gabi felt the noose getting tighter and tighter, the web getting thicker and thicker. Yet, she neither had the will and nor the patience to fight any longer. She simply gave up and remained submissive and obedient, like a trained puppy.

Many a times, she wished that she were dead. She would think that, were she to commit suicide, what the best way would be. Whatever way, it had to cause the least pain, and had to be one hundred percent. She didn't want to be left paralyzed or crippled.

She thought of jumping in front of a speeding car, But what about the guilt that the innocent driver would have to live with all his life? Also there would be the problem of her mother's feelings towards the driver, not to mention the public condemnations and the prosecutions.

Another way would be to jump from a tall building. It would have to be tall enough to ensure certain death. But she had learned in church that the human body was the temple of God and, as such, should be well taken care of. Also, she had read that in many religions suicide was regarded as a sin. What if the Creator would send her back to relive her life as a punishment?

The best way, she thought, was to be killed for a just cause. For example, she could intercede in a quarrel, as Tybalt did, and be killed accidentally. But what were the chances of finding such an opportunity? But just the fact that she was seeking this opportunity would make it a sin and defeat the purpose.

So, the only option that remained was to die naturally and withstand the fortunes or misfortunes of life.

On Monday, she went back to work as usual. She was engaged in her computer work when she noticed a young man approaching her desk.

He appeared as if he had come from nowhere. Suddenly, he was standing in front of her. He seemed to be in his late thirties. He had an olive complexion, with neck-long black hair, parted in the middle. He looked quite smart in his black jacket, white open-collared shirt, and double cuffed linen trousers. He was slim and about six foot tall, quite handsome, she thought.

"Can I help you?" she offered.

"My name is Greg and I have an appointment to discuss a project with Daniel."

"What time is your appointment?"

"Ten o'clock."

"It's only quarter to. I'm sure Daniel will be on time. May I get you a cup of coffee in the meantime?"

That's the physical appearance of a man I would like in my life, she thought. She decided to engage him in conversation and maybe find out more about him. Luckily, her colleagues had taken a coffee break and there was no one around. She had another stroke of luck as her boss called to say he would be half an hour late.

She found out that Greg was single. He had come from another city with a chance for a job in Daniel's company as a lighting designer and would move, provided he got the job. His tone of voice and smile seemed to suggest that he might be interested in her, but she wasn't sure. It was only a woman's feelings.

Greg did get the job and as time passed, he asked Gabi for a date. The relationship developed and eventually Gabi went to live with Greg.

She kept her job and her irregular hours of work but Greg was not bothered. In fact, his own hours were so inconsistent that he would have to inform Gabi each evening whether he could make it to dinner or not. She never knew where he was and when questioned, he would reply "designer hours are irregular and inconsistent."

But Gabi didn't complain. Unmarried couples always have to make that special effort and she had to be on her toes till the day Greg would pop the question, especially since her mother kept nagging her about the immoral life she was living.

More and more, she was noticing peculiarities about Greg. Most important of all was the fact that he was not talkative, much less now that they were living together. She kept wondering if he had secret interests that he did not want to reveal. At the same time, nothing seemed to upset or irritate him. He had a serenity within him that was quite visible in his eyes and complexion. He only slept a few hours every night, if at all, but was never tired. If she would by chance wake up in the middle of the night to go to the loo or get a drink of water, he would be awake. After a while, Gabi didn't ask any questions but kept wondering about the eerie quality in Greg.

Once a month, Gabi and Greg would go to Cornelia on a Saturday evening for dinner and sometimes they would sleep over. Cornelia would give up her bed and sleep on the sofa. Sunday morning they would all go to church after eating breakfast. Then the couple would leave.

One evening when Gabi and Greg were watching TV, Gabi decided that she must muster all her courage and determination to have an in-depth conversation with Greg about the direction of her life.

"Greg," she began, "I had a dream last night and you know that I never have dreams. My grandmother came to me and told me that we must get married and go to live abroad. She said that we would be having two little boys."

Greg cut her short. "Dreams are non-sense. Mabe you slept on a full stomach. Dreams are extensions of your waking hours".

"But what about the Bible? What about Jacob?"

"That is pure folklore. These were stories narrated from generation lto generation for entertainment purposes."

"Greg, you don't believe in dreams. Do you believe in afterlife?"

"Not in the same way you do. I don't believe in a Day of Judgement when the souls wake up, or in punishment and reward. Do you really want to know what I believe in? It may contradict all your religious beliefs."

"Very much so,"

"I believe, as most astrologers now know, that the universe is infinite with unlimited solar systems. Once you die, just as you came to this planet, you will go to another one. But there are two problems. One is Time. You could be born millions or billions of years in the future or in the past. The other is Kind. You could be born as anything animate, depending on where you are born.

"You mean a reptile or a bacteria or anything unknown to us on earth.

"Precisely. Even a unit of energy."

"So you think there is life on other planets?"

"Of course, stupid. So you see, there is no chance at all of your grandma coming to you in your sleep,"

"Then, according to your theory, two beings living concurrently on this planet are destined never to meet again. That's very scary. I'd rather not think of it at all."

"The chances are next to zero. So, all that is left for humans is to enjoy every second of life with all their senses. Many poets have written about this but it's physically impossible to do. You must think that you are doing everything that you do for the last time."

They fell silent, each immersed in his own thoughts.

Gabi realized that Greg was never going to marry her and she didn't want to have children without marriage. It didn't look like he wanted children anyway. It wasn't a subject for discussion. But what were her options? She would either have to continue living with Greg or she had to go back living with her mother. Of the two options, she preferred the first. Time would temper Greg.

"I also believe," Greg continued, "that matter amalgamated with energy can be transferred. Anything or anyone can be disintegrated into almost energized invisible particles and reinstated in a different area."

"You mean from country to country?"

"Even from one solar system to another."

"What about the soul, then? Can it also be moved from place to place or do you believe that there is no such thing as a soul?" Fearing what he might answer, she added, "every religion, past and present, believes in the existence of the soul."

"I personally do not believe in the existence of a soul simply because if you relocate animate matter, then you have to inject a soul into it. If we clone an animate matter, who will inject the soul?"

Gabi did not want to continue the discussion. Greg had read too much science fiction. Or, he was just toying with ideas he had heard about.

More and more, Gabi started thinking about her relation-ship with Greg. He was very considerate and caring and he was always cheerful. He always addressed Gabi with "dear" or "darling" but there was something missing and strange. She couldn't exactly pinpoint it but it seemed that Greg was void of all human emotions and feelings. What she was seeing was put-ons that could fool everyone, but not Gabi. His endurance and strength also seemed out of the ordinary.

Her sex life also seemed mechanical "Lets go to bed," she would offer, slowly walking towards the bedroom. She would wait for him to undress her and lay her on the bed. But as that did not happen, she would undress herself and put her arms round his neck, pulling him to the bed. She would expect him to massage her to a climax but there was no foreplay. He simply did his thing mechanically and moved away, somewhat like monkeys do in the zoo.

One evening, Gabi decided to confront him. After dinner, when they had nestled down to watch TV, she made him a cup of tea and sat on the sofa beside him. When the ads came, she gently turned his chin towards her.

"You can talk as we watch," he murmured, turning his face back to the TV screen.

"No, it's serious. Can we turn the TV off for a few minutes?"

"Sure." He replied, switching the TV off.

Never a friction, objection, or disagreement, she thought. Well, let's see what he's got to say now.

"I mean, I'm not getting any younger and soon I won't be able to bear healthy children, if at all. To have children, we have to get married as I don't want to have children out of wedlock."

Silence. It felt as if a rat was gnawing her guts, but she continued.

"My mother is also upset and tells me that I'm living an immoral life with an atheist."

"I don't want any children, not now anyway," Greg answered curtly "Consider us, in your mind, as married. Do you necessarily need a marriage certificate?"

Her hopes were dashed but she thought it would be better for her to keep the peace for the time being. She had no choice.

As time passed, she became more and more irritable and aggressive. The relationship was becoming unbearable. She tried to suppress her emotions and knew that Greg was aware of all this. She waited for him to make a move.

Then, one evening Greg proposed to take her to "a quiet dinner so we can get to discuss things."

They sat on a candle-lit table in the corner of a pub, ordering beer and spaghetti. They chatted about everyday trivial things. Gabi was concerned that they had not gone to stay with her mother for some time now and Greg promised that they would do so on Saturday and attend church services on Sunday.

Much to Gabi's displeasure, the conversation drifted into what she believed to be science fiction. Greg was in one of those moods again and she had no choice but to put up with it.

"Do you love me, Gabi?"

"What a silly question. Of course, I do."

"But again, what is 'love'? It's not merely a physical attraction. Perhaps, I should us the word 'like.' If "love" is some kind of spiritual union, then I don't know if it exists. Most probably it doesn't exist and souls don't exist either."

"Can you please change the subject?" Gabi said sorely. "It's such a beautiful and peaceful evening."

"I know that 'like' exists. It's like the attraction of the north and south poles of a magnet. Gabi, I've never known you to engage in deep conversation. Can't you stretch your imagination a little? Stretch it like a rubber band."

"I'll try if it makes you happy."

"So, if I 'like' you and you 'like' me, which I know you do, will you come with me wherever I go? We could go beyond the stars, where life exist as units of energy and everything happens in impulses."

"Are you mad? Are you dreaming? The books you are reading are making you kookoo. Wake up, Mr Superman, we are back on earth."

"Sex would be through impulses and a new unit of energy created. Communication would be through waves and there would be no need for food or sleep. Will you come with me?"

"Yes, yes. I'll come with you. But right now let's not talk any more. Let's go home. You need to relax a bit and maybe you'll feel better."

In the following weeks Gabi wondered who to go to for help. She talked to her mother regarding Greg's deranged state of mind and wondered if her mother would ask her boss, the dentist, to recommend a psychiatrist of psychoanalyst. Everything had to be done on the quiet so that the news would not leak out to friends and relatives.

Greg, of course, must have realized what was going on in Gabi's mind and he decided to act normal, ceasing all conversation that might cause her tension.

Life continued and another six months passed without incident.

One Saturday morning, Gabi woke up with severe abdominal pain together with convulsions. The pain was so excruciating that Greg decided not to wait for an ambulance. Instead, he picked up Gabi, carried her to the elevator and to the parking lot in the basement of the building. He laid her on the back seat of his Honda station and sped to the hospital via the highway.

He appeared to be very nervous and was desperate to reach the hospital. The speedometer climbed from 70 miles an hour to 100 miles. He overtook a Range Rover to his right and turned his head to the backseat to see if Gabi was okay.

The next thing that was heard was a thunderous explosion. A head-on collision had occurred with a black Mercedes speeding from the opposite direction.

Traffic came to a standstill as drivers and occupants poured out of their cars. A bald man in his fifties called the ambulance service. Another driver called the police.

The driver of the Mercedes, an athletic man in his twenties, came out of his car and rushed to the Honda. Miraculously, he had only suffered bruises and cuts, thanks to his airbag, but was otherwise unaffected.

The bonnet of the Honda was wrinkled like an accordion and the bumper had fallen to the ground. Engine pieces and radiator pieces were scattered everywhere. The windscreen was also shattered and Greg could be seen, unconscious and bleeding from the head as he lay trapped behind the wheel. Gabi was also unconscious or probably dead, being dislodged from the back-seat onto the rear floor of the car. Her arms and ribs were broken and she didn't seem to be breathing.

The wailing sirens could be heard in the distance. A crowd had gathered round the Honda with people trying to free Greg from the wreckage.

The police arrived shortly. They pushed the crowd back and cordoned the section of the highway where the Mercedes and Honda lay. All the uninjured people were ordered to return and stay in their vehicles until the highway could be cleared and the ambulance would arrive. The injured people were taken to the side of the road.

It was almost noon now and the clouds that were gathering all morning enshrouded the accident site. Then came thunder, lightning and torrents of rain. It became pitch black and visibility was reduced to almost nothing. The policemen also rushed to the sanctuary of their cars, waiting for the storm to subside.

The ambulances arrived but they also had to wait for the weather to clear.

An hour passed.

When the clouds lifted, the police and ambulance crew approached the accident site. To their amazement, the Honda together with its occupants had disappeared. The highway was sparkling clean with no trace of any debris. The Mercedes, however, remained in its place with no sign of an accident. The driver was behind the wheel, fast asleep.

A search was immediately ordered. The hospitals across the country were given descriptions of Greg and Gabi but nothing was found.

The story was all over the mass media for the next month but as time passed everything was forgotten. All that remained was a myth, a folklore to be passed on to the next generations, just as stories of aliens and UFOs are.

Cornelia had not heard anything that Saturday. As she expected Gabi and Greg that evening, she busily tidied the flat and cooked the dinner. She laid the table for three, glanced at her watch and muttered, "they should be here any minute."

A SECOND CHANCE

My name is Robert Westend.

I want to tell you my story in plain, simple language, the language of the commoner. For, in my opinion, that's the best way to communicate. Surely, you will not need a dictionary by your side and definitely no computer.

By most people's standards, I was a very handsome young man. I was 5'10" tall, broad shouldered, but slightly obese. Pleasingly plump, you might say. I had a head full of dark brown hair which I combed from my forehead to the back of my neck and when I wore my designer suit, I seemed to be irresistible to all the pretty girls around me.

Or maybe it wasn't the clothes or my looks. Maybe it was my wealth. As my surname suggests, my family were aristocrats, whatever that is supposed to mean, from the West End of London. We were not developers of property, but we certainly seemed to own quite a few freehold properties, primarily in central London.

So, I had no worries in life. I would wake up when I woke up and my breakfast would be ready. My chauffeur would be at hand to take me around and, as he lived on our estate, was at my service any time I needed him.

I would pop into our offices once a week just to show the staff that I was around. We had forty staff members in our building working on property maintenance, collection of rents, eviction of tenants etc.

The only other person who stood to benefit from our family fortune was my sister Glenda. At 29, she was three years older than me and still single.

No one seemed to be good enough for her. A description of her is not necessary except to say that she was a fairly good looking blonde. Perhaps it was our lifestyle that kept her from looking for a husband.

We spent the time with friends in our league, people like us who were wealthy and aimless enough to lead a Carpe Diem life, travelling, shopping, and eating out. Most of our nights, of course, were spent in trendy nightclubs and discos.

Sunday, May 26th, was cloudy and dark all day long. Towards the evening there were heavy showers and it didn't seem that it would clear up at all. I was feeling a bit lethargic and since the weather was so gloomy anyway, I decided to call it an early night and went to sleep around 10 p.m.

I woke up in a sweat at about 4 a.m. I felt as if a lorry had parked on my chest with pain in my neck and shoulders. I recognized the symptoms as that of a heart attack and quickly pressed the bell to the side of the bed.

I must have passed out since the next thing I remembered was myself in the hospital. I was paralyzed from the waist down. I had no feelings in my arms and could not move them. My knuckles folded into my hands and just looking at them disgusted me.

I was like a Ferrari that had been totalled on the highway. Life no longer seemed to be worth living and I wanted to be dead. I prayed for death all the time. The only escape was sleep and every night before I finally drifted into sleep, I would pray that, should God be gracious to me, I would not wake up again.

My friends and I used to joke about wealth, "what's the use of wealth if you don't have health?" But what if you don't have both? At least the wealth could bring some convenience and some comfort.

I was brought back to our Chelsea home. The maids would talk to me as they cleaned my room each morning but I always seemed to be far away, lost in my thoughts and dreams of the past and how my friends forsook me. I had a special cook whose only job was to cook exotic foods for me each day.

As I slightly recuperated, my sister did her utmost to keep me entertained and to bring some kind of meaning to my life. She would take me to the theatre at least once a month and also to the opera which I hated but put up with in order not to annoy her.

On Thursday nights I would be taken to a casino on Berkley Square in our limousine and Paul, our driver, would wheel me to a roulette table. Glenda would bring a couple of her girlfriends and, of course, my private nurse would always be at hand.

Nearly prostate on my wheelchair, I observed everything and everyone around me but I wasn't interested in the game. What difference did it make to me what number would come or who would win or lose? The expressions and the emotional outbursts of the gamblers were far more interesting and I concentrated on the players rather than on the game.

For the last six months, I had noticed a slender man, probably in his late thirties, dressed in a black suit but without a tie, making the rounds of the tables in the casino. He would always end up standing beside my wheelchair. He was always alone, never spoke to anyone and never gambled.

My eyes would follow him round the room as he hesitated on some of the roulette tables, watching the ball as it rested on a number. His head was balding and he wore black rimmed glasses but he had no features that would make him stand out or be noticed. Neither did he show any emotion at any time.

On Thursday evening, as my chauffeur pushed my wheelchair to the roulette table close to the entrance of the casino, I noticed him standing by a table. He stood behind the gathered players, keeping a distance from them. My wheelchair went past him to the table and Paul asked the players to make room for me. They moved slightly from my right and left, making room for the wheelchair. Maybe they pitied me but I felt that most couldn't care less. At the same time, I noticed the black suited man take two steps forward, so that he stood to the right of my wheelchair. My sister was standing to my left with a handful of ten pound chips.

"What number shall we put on, Robert?" she asked childishly.

I didn't answer as I couldn't have cared less.

"Let's put one chip on 29 which is my birthday and one chip on 12, which is your birthday.

I noticed that the man in black was eying me and I returned his gaze. We were fixated for about a minute, then all of a sudden he grabbed both of my limp hands which were resting by my thighs and commanded, "get up Robert. Let's take a walk."

I couldn't believe what was happening. He started yanking me out of the wheelchair and my sister, in a state of shock, started screaming at the top of her lungs, "hey what do you think you are doing, you madman? Leave him the fuck alone." She screamed for the security guards and Paul went off, looking for the security guards. The casino guests gathered and there was chaos and pandemonium.

In the commotion, the black suited man had already unseated me and positioned my left arm round his shoulders. He then put his right arm round my waist and holding my left arm with his left hand, he yanked me out of the wheelchair.

As my feet hit the ground, I felt a gush of blood flow from my waist to my toes. Another gush of blood went from my heart to the tip of my fingers. Feeling was being restored to all parts of my body.

No words can explain what I felt, nor can any human comprehend such a feeling unless he experiences it himself, so that, to attempt to describe it would prove futile. Finally, walking on my own, I kept thinking that I would soon wake up from my dream. I was never a believer in miracles and never believed that any Saint had performed a miracle. Even Lazarus must have had some kind of sleeping sickness.

The casino had come to a standstill. The gamblers had stopped gambling and seemed mesmerized. The security was trying to penetrate the crowd surrounding me, although, seeing me on my feet, they kept a fair distance away as if repelled by a magnet of fear. Foreign guests were shouting and yelling to each other, and it reminded me of the Tower of Babel.

But soon calm was restored and the gaming continued. Perhaps people thought that I was not a cripple after all but was recuperating from a malady of some kind. All except those who knew me well, of course.

We walked the full round of the casino floor and some guests seemed to follow, always keeping a distance. My sister followed close to our heels. Although she was numb with shock, she had calmed down considerably.

We made our way to a sofa and cold water was brought to me. I looked into the face of the gentleman in black who was seated next to me and all else became a blur.

"Who, in God's name, are you? Are you a prophet or an alien? Please tell me before I have another heart attack."

"My name is Jeremy, short for Jeremiah," he answered in a voice that was hardly audible.

"You must be some kind of miracle worker, some kind of Jesus. I have got to get to know you. But what can I do for you? Obviously, you are not after money but how can I repay you? Just tell me." I could only ask in spurts as the excitement and exhaustion had taken my breath away.

No expression or emotion appeared on his face.

"I tell you what...." he said.

"What?" I echoed.

"Go to the cashier and cash two hundred pounds. Take the two hundred pounds to the nearest roulette table and put it on number eight."

"Done."

"You will get seven thousand pounds. Then go to another table. Put one thousand pounds, which is the maximum bet, on number twenty nine and call out 'twenty nine and neighbours by two hundred.' That should net you fourty three thousand two hundred pounds. That is my fee. I will be sitting here and watching you as you play."

After my miraculous cure, I felt that nothing was impossible. I made my way to the cashiers but was aware of the crowd which included two managers, following me. I could also hear the buzz and commotion of the crowd in the background. I looked back to check the whereabouts of Jeremy and saw that he was still sitting on the sofa, now a lone figure.

I cashed the two hundred pounds and went to a high stake table which was empty. 'Minimum thousand pounds' it read. I put the two hundred pounds on number eight and was not at all surprised when the number came up.

Again I looked back to make sure that Jeremy was waiting for me. He was still sitting on the sofa where I had left him with the glass of water in his hand. I made the thumbs up sign and he responded with a nod.

I proceeded to the next table and did as I was instructed. There was never a doubt in my mind that number twenty nine would come up as it did. The crowd shouted "well done," and 'yes, yes."

I looked at Jeremy and waved, then went straight to the cashiers. I cashed my chips and headed toward the sofa where Jeremy was sitting but he was not there. The sofa was occupied by other casino guests.

Well, I thought, Jeremy must have gotten tired of sitting and was probably standing by a table and watching as he always used to do or maybe trying to find me. Unable to find him, I was getting nervous and frustrated. Then my mobile rang.

"It's Jeremy."

"Where are you? I've looked everywhere for you."

"You have had the gift of a second chance." The phone went dead.

I tried to find his number on my phone, but there was nothing. Nothing had registered on the call history.

I rushed to the sofa where he had been sitting and asked the occupants if they had seen a man dressed in a black suit with Jeremy's description. No one had seen anything. I proceeded to the front desk and they assured me that no one with Jeremy's description had entered or left the casino. They insisted that no one could bypass them and that they knew all the guests. Furthermore, they had photos of all who entered. The doorman too swore that he had not seen anyone with that description. He swore because I had become aggressive.

We then decided to come back the next morning, when it would be relatively quiet, to check the identity of Jeremy.

I didn't even bother going to bed that night and neither did my sister or chauffeur. I paced the living room as we discussed everything. We traced and retraced every minute and every step till restlessness and fatigue drove us to sit down and doze off time and again.

Eight in the morning, I had a triple shot of espresso in an effort to keep my wits about me. I looked at the wall clock time and again till it blurred into the wrinkled clock of Salvadore Dali.

Finally, at ten o'clock, we drove down to the casino. The receptionists knew what we wanted but claimed that clients' details were confidential and could not be revealed. That's what the lady with the reddish, close cropped hair, and clementine size boobs told me. We knew that we could get nowhere with her and asked for her manager.

Her male colleague was more receptive, especially when I put a bundle of 50 pound notes in his pocket.

Jeremy was an odd name. In fact, there was only one Jeremy in the computer system and as the photo with details came up, I immediately recognized him. "That's him," I shouted in excitement. My sister nudged me and whispered to keep my voice down. I asked for a printout but my request was denied. "Write down what you want," the manager said.

We sped to Jeremy's address in North London where he was supposed to have a furniture business.

The premises were gated and looked like a detached mansion. We drove through the gates and parked.

I rushed through the door and found a receptionist in front of me. I asked her for the manager's office, supposing that to be Jeremy's. She pointed to a door at the back of the showroom and I rushed towards it.

Anxiously, I knocked on the door but couldn't wait for an answer. As I pushed the door open, I was almost pissing in my pants with excitement.

It was not Jeremy who was sitting behind the desk in the room. Instead it was a muscular man, in his early thirties, with a shaven head, immaculately dressed in a blue suit and red tie.

"I'm looking for Jeremy Shepherd."

"What's your business with him?"

"I'm a friend, a close friend," I blurted.

"You can't be a close friend of his if you haven't seen him for seven years. Jeremy died of a heart attack seven years ago. Is there anything I can help you with?"

I froze with shock and bewilderment. "It can't be, it's impossible. He was in the casino with us last night."

I gave him a physical description to make sure we were talking about the same person.

"Your description is exact," the young man said. "I should well know what he looked like. You see, Jeremy was my father."

"Could you please let me know where he is buried?"

"At Edgewarebury Cemetery. Go to row thirteen and it's the fifth grave."

I didn't wait to hear more. Off we went to the cemetery and sure enough, we found his grave with the inscription:

JEREMY SHEPHERD
BORN 1924—DIED DECEMBER 15, 1984

I am compelled to tell my tale, however trivial, as did the ancient mariner. However, I wonder about the countless souls who travel this planet. Will they have a second chance?

THE PARASITE

Those who knew him called him the parasite, "El Parasito." They would converse saying, El Parasito did this or El Parasito said that. Perhaps, to their amusement, the word "EL" reminded them ironically of the majestic character of the El Matadors whose attributes the parasite believed he possessed.

Herbert was born to a lower middle class family. His father was a commission agent who would go to various companies or people and try to sell them something: tea from India, cloth from Hong Kong or cigarette lighters. He carried a small suitcase with samples and barely managed to make a living.

Herbert, however, was put in the best school his parents could afford. It was very important to them that he should receive the best education their money could buy. Most important, he had to master the English language. Eloquence and articulation meant almost everything. "The tongue, the tongue," his father would say. "It's only a piece of meat but it's capable of almost anything. Look at the top lawyers in this country or any country for that matter. Why are they so successful? Because they have mastered the tongue. They can convince you of almost anything. They can convince you that black is white and white is black, day is night and night is day."

The other important thing that was instilled into Herbert's being by his parents was that he should try to take advantage of everything and everyone around him.

"Do not waste your time with people who have nothing or little to offer," his father would say. " Just shrug them off but do not be rude to them either."

"I'll give you an example of an event that occurred in my childhood. Two of my classmates were very close to each other during their sophomore and senior years in high school. One of them was called Morris and the other Daniel. Their parents were from the same community and they socialized together. I mean, they were real close to each other and so were the kids."

"Maurice and Daniel made a vow to each other. They promised each other that should either of them fail in business in their lifetime and be really in need, the other would help bail him out."

"Well they graduated and went into business, each on his own. They got married and had children but they still occasionally socialized together as had their parents."

"It was funny that, while they were both in the same business, Morris was doing extremely well but Daniel was living from hand to mouth. Morris became a prominent merchant and was known in the whole market. He bought a palatial home and had servants to wait on him and cooks to cook for him. He bought a few carriages with fine horses and had a servant to take him to work and stay with him all day. Obviously in those days there were no cars."

"Then it happened that one of Daniel's customers who owed Daniel a considerable amount of money became bankrupt and as a result Daniel could not pay his suppliers."

"Daniel did not want to turn to Morris for help but he had no choice. He finally gathered enough courage to visit Morris and he had no doubts that Morris would help him."

"So one afternoon Daniel showed up at Morris's door. He knew that Morris would be home as it was the custom for businesses to close at noontime and to reopen in the afternoon. You could call that the Siesta Time."

"Morris welcomed Daniel into his house. He asked the servants to serve him with food and drink and finally asked Daniel the reason for his visit as it had been a year or more since he had seen him last."

"Daniel then told him of his problems. He reminded him of their vows to each other in their schooldays and told him that if he was not helped, he would also go bankrupt."

"Morris did not reply. Instead, he casually turned the conversation to different subjects. Daniel would keep on hinting but to no avail. Morris always avoided the subject."

"Daniel was racked with nervousness and tension. He wanted the time to pass so he could go home. The market would open again at four but he had nothing to go back to. Better to go home and sit in his room for the rest of the evening before facing the creditors the next morning."

"Finally, Daniel blurted out that he wanted to go home but Morris insisted that he would take him in his carriage. As they both sat in the carriage, Morris told the driver to take Daniel home but to first go through the market and past his office."

"This they did and then they dropped Daniel by his house. Not a word about assistance, Daniel thought. When you go down, no one wants to know, not even your best friends."

"The next morning Daniel reluctantly went to his store in the market. He was prepared to face an agonizing day as he walked through the market. Already from far he could see one of his suppliers, to whom he owed money approaching him. I have no choice but to face him and all those who will definitely come, he thought"

"However, much to his surprise, the supplier pleasantly greeted Daniel. He told Daniel that he understood that sometimes merchants could have financial trouble and agreed to extend the date of his credit."

"Others came and even though Daniel owed them money, they offered to supply him more goods."

"So, now Daniel understood that through the tour that Morris had given him, Morris had lived up to his promise."

Herbert was fascinated. His father's story had an immense effect on him and he decided to live his life in accordance with the essence of the story. Stick to the rich and influential and ignore the poor but do not to disrespect them.

Besides the rich and influential, Herbert was to stick to his immediate family. The immediate family was of utmost importance, meaning his mother and father and his sisters and brothers. Everybody else was to be shunned except, of course, the SUPER RICH.

After graduation from high school, Herbert went to work as a sales assistant for a firm exporting machinery to the Middle East. He lived with his parents and saved all his salary and commissions. He seldom went out, trying to save as much money as he could. "Money" was the key to power and everything else that would come with it.

As the years passed, his parents started looking for a wife for him within their social circles. His wife would have to come from a good family and above all, the girl's parents had to be rich enough to afford a good dowry to enable Herbert to buy a little house or, at least, a flat. Herbert didn't mind arranged marriages. As a matter of fact he preferred it. At least with arranged marriages, the girl would be from a good family with proper upbringing. There was also a very good chance she would be a virgin.

It would be wonderful to marry a virgin. Many a times, Herbert would dream about marrying a virgin! "Virgin! Virgin! Virgin!" He most certainly needed a Virgin. He started fantasizing about Virgins. He would create fictitious girls in his mind and dream and how he would be the first man in their lives."

Of course the big bonus with a Virgin would be that she would not have experienced the size of a man's penis and indeed the pleasures that would be derived from it. He was quite concerned since he was quite sure that he had a small penis.

So, Herbert's mother took it upon herself to find her son a suitable bride. Of utmost importance to her was to find her son a humble woman. She would have to be easily dominated and subservient. It would be difficult to find such a girl in this day and age, but she would certainly give it a go. She just didn't want anyone who would give the least of hassle to her darling son.

An extremely religious girl would have all the attributes but that wouldn't do either. The orthodox families were to be avoided as Herbert would never adhere to their practices. Perhaps she could find a girl whose parents were old fashioned and strict but not particularly religious. Her parents would have to be strict in the sense of not allowing their daughter to go out with anyone unless it was with the intention of marriage. Finding such a girl would be like winning the lottery.

The years rolled on. Herbert saved most of his salary and commissions and only went out with girls to mess about, nothing serious. Meanwhile, his mother kept on looking for a marriageable girl. She was very conscious of the fact that her son was now 28 years old and had to get married soon.

Then one evening at a wedding party Herbert's mother, Daisy, was seated next to a friend whom she had not seen for years.

"Well, hello Daisy," Sarah said excitedly. "Imagine, our sitting next to each other after all these years of not having seen each other. How have you been?"

"Quite well," Daisy replied.

The conversation drifted every which way and finally they focused on the important matters, being the children.

"Is Herbert married yet," Sarah asked?

"As a matter of fact, I am very concerned about Herbert in regards to his settling down. He has a fine job and he is saving all his money but he still lives with us."

"What is wrong with that?"

"Nothing. Except we are hoping that somehow he will meet the right girl and somehow settle down."

"Somehow? There are so many unmarried girls in our circles."

"Yes but my Herbert is a little different than most young men in the sense that he is old-fashioned in his taste for girls."

"How so?"

"He is looking for, how shall I best put it….., for….. a kind of homely girl. A girl who will be a good housewife and, more or less be obedient to him. She also has to be from a good family."

"Well that shouldn't be difficult to find."

"But that's not all. Herbert is looking for a girl whose parents would be capable of helping him buy a flat."

"In other words, they have to be rich and give her a good dowry."

"You got it."

"I tell you what," Sarah said excitedly. "My daughter Florence would be a good match for your son Herbert. She is now 22 years old and having finished high school, she helps me at home. We are not filthy rich but my husband is generous enough to help them out with a flat."

"Doesn't Florence work at all?

"She works part –time at the local library which is just on the high road."

"There certainly is nothing to lose. Give me Florence's mobile and I'll ask Herbert to give her a call."

And so, they went out for about a month. Herbert felt that Florence was the sort of girl he would want to marry. She wasn't particularly good-looking, just ordinary. She was brunette, slim, about five foot eight, not the sort of girl anyone would turn round to look at twice. But she seemed to have all the qualities and attributes that Herbert was looking for. She tried to bear a smile all the time she was with him and hardly objected to anything. She seemed to be humble to the point of being subservient and that was what Herbert was looking for.

Herbert had to remember what his father Neil had taught him throughout the years: "be reserved and distant. Once you get too close to people, your emotions start playing up," his father would insist. "Always listen to your head and never to your heart."

Before picking up Florence for a date, Herbert would ring her up on his mobile and ask her to stand outside the entrance to the apartments. He would rather not go up to the flat as familiarity could soften him towards Florence's family. Better to remain distant and less familiar. Herbert's father had told him that this sort of behaviour would gain him much more respect. Who knows? Perhaps he was right.

Florence, on the other hand, fell head over heels in love with Herbert. He was objective and knew what he wanted in life. He was more head than heart, 80 percent head would not be an exaggeration. He was stubborn and domineering and Florence was happy enough to take the back seat. Perhaps for her it would be less of a responsibility in life, being the passenger instead of the driver.

Soon it was time to make the necessary arrangements for an engagement and Florence's parents invited Herbert and his parents for dinner. As they were parking outside the apartment block, Neil reminded Herbert that he should in no way get involved in the conversation regarding the dowry.

After dinner both families retired to the living room, seating themselves on the sofas. Suspense was in the air as both families knew what was to be discussed next.

Being quite shy and timid, Florence did not venture into the living room but made her way to the kitchen, out of sight.

Neil shared the same sofa as Florence's father, Samuel, while Herbert took a seat at the far corner of the room, perhaps to give an impression of detachablity in case the conversation heated up.

Sarah and Daisy sat on the chairs in the middle of the room and anxiously awaited the main subject, being that of the dowry, to commence as it finally did.

"Well," Neil began, "I presume that we will be doing the engagement party but, as it is customary, you will be responsible for the wedding ceremony."

"We will be happy to take care of the wedding ceremony," Samuel responded.

"Yes, and we have to insist that it must be held at a most reputable hotel," Neil said forcefully .

Samuel thought it would not be wise not to respond and let matters be till later.

Neil carried on in a vociferous tone, "As regards, the dowry, you are pretty well aware that my son does not have a flat and the married couple must have a decent place to live."

"Yes, my wife did mention this to me and I will be most happy to help as much as I can."

"The problem is, before we can go any further, how much can you donate? Forgive me for being blunt, but it's better to go straight to the point."

"I want to help as much as I can. After all, they are both my children but right now all I can manage is £200,000."

"That's nothing. You can't even buy a barn for that money, let alone a decent flat. We need at least £500,000."

"I'm sure your son Herbert must have saved something and they can always get a mortgage."

"That's neither here nor there," Neil replied emphatically.

"I'm afraid that's all I can do right now," Samuel replied resignedly.

"Well," Neil said rising to his feet, "as this is not going to work out, we are very sorry to have troubled you."

He lowered his head to avoid looking at anyone and headed towards the door. His wife and son hurriedly rose to their feet as if given a cue and followed as puppies follow their mother. Their faces bore no emotion or expression

As the door of the flat closed behind them, Florence broke out in tears and rushed to the living room where her parents were still sitting dazed with the outcome.

"What bastards," she sobbed. "I at least, expected Herbert to say something. Anything. He doesn't have any feelings for me. That's what it is."

"Maybe he didn't want to oppose his father," Samuel said dejectedly.

"Even though he doesn't display much emotion, I still love him. Is there any way we can raise the money?"

"It is too much to raise and I'm sure, with the way they have treated us, Neil is not going to budge in the least."

Sarah joined them, sobbingly imploring her husband: "Samuel, please do something. After all, her happiness is at stake."

"It doesn't look as if they will negotiate and don't forget that we still have to pay for the wedding ceremony, the band, and everything else that comes with it."

"I know but what choice do we have? We will have to get a mortgage on our flat."

"But we have to consider our other daughter and our son," Samuel said reluctantly.

Samuel's wife, together with Florence, nagged their father incessantly. Samuel had no choice but to mortgage his flat in order to pay for the dowry and wedding expenses and this left him heavily in debt.

What Samuel and his family did not realize and which only time would unfold, was the web that this parasitical spider (if there exists such a creature) was to spin around himself and his immediate family so as to shut out all other humanoids. That is, except for the extremely affluent.

From the outset, Herbert made it clear that with the exception of his immediate family, no one was welcome in his house. His immediate family consisted of his parents, his sister and his brother together with their children. Florence protested, but to no avail. She asked her husband why her parents and their children were exempted to which Herbert responded that she could go out to see them any time she pleased and on certain occasions they could be invited for dinner but that, under no circumstances, were they to pop in unannounced.

To this effect, Herbert created THE SATURDAY DINNER even though he was not particularly religious. This would be an occasion where his immediate family would gather around themselves and where, maybe once a month, Florence could invite her parents over.

A good insight into the Herbert's character was his interaction with guests from different levels of society who would come to a wedding reception. Herbert would enter the jam packed reception room with the intention of mingling with the most wealthy guests. After all, what was he to gain from the poor ones? From the rich ones, he might get a lead or a tip on a stock or maybe just information.

Guests who were not well off, in the sense that they didn't have much wealth or much of a prospect of acquiring some, were to be totally avoided. After all, what was the sense of talking to them? That would just be a waste of time. Herbert would swerve this way and that way in order to totally avoid them.

A short nod of recognition would be sufficient for those guests who were better off. These might be the guests who were salaried and therefore wouldn't have the opportunity of acquiring much wealth.

The rest of Herbert's time would be dedicated proportionately to guests who were affluent. The more affluent you were, the more time would be dedicated to you.

And if you were at the top, there you would find Herbert most of the evening. He would be ass- kissing like it was no one's business. "What would you like?" he would say. "Can I get you a drink?" "Is your mother alright?" Of course he didn't give a damn about the guy's mother. Herbert had learned that intimate questions of concern or sympathy were bound to soften the bastard into parting with information which he wouldn't be likely to do under normal circumstances.

But above all, was his immediate family. Were he to see his sister or brother who had also been invited to the same wedding, he would stick to them like glue. Even though he had been with them the evening before, it was as if he hadn't seen them for ten years.

Herbert kept to his special principles. Florence's parents were not allowed to visit and nor were her nieces and nephews. They simply were not rich enough and nor was there anything to gain from them. At the outset, Florence protested but to no avail.

"Why don't you want my parents to come over. What have you got against them?"

"Don't ever raise your voice when speaking to me. Your parents are welcome but only when we invite them. They are not welcome to pop in when they please."

"But they are never invited. Your side of the family comes here every Saturday night for dinner but my side of the family is outlawed. That's not fair."

"Nothing is fair in this world. I'm only looking for the interests of our family. We have no time to waste on people."

"They are not "people." They are my family and if yours are dear to you, then mine are dear to me."

"Well that's the way its going to be whether you like it or not. If not, then you're welcome to leave."

Florence was not about to leave. She would simply have to see her parents when Herbert was at work and she believed that they would understand. Divorce would bring complications which she could simply not go through. At best, she would have to live with her parents. How long would she bear to do that? And what about finding a job? Her conscience would not permit her to live off her parents.

And worst of all, what about finding another soul-mate. Soul? What a joke. Florence was religious only in name. Rituals and ceremonies fascinated her only in a social sense. She loved gossip and made it her business to find out all that was going on in her social circle.

But as to finding another husband, that would be out of the question. Divorced women were frowned upon, especially if they were not women of means.

Besides the mental anguish, which she hoped would not last, she had a comfortable life. She had a daily maid who came in the mornings to help her with the daily chores and she was free in the afternoons to socialize. She could call up her parents and take them for a coffee or she could call up her wealthy friends to socialize, whether it be for lunch or to visit boutiques.

She had ample money. Her husband gave her what she wanted. He wanted her to look at her best. She would visit her hairdresser once a week and would manicure and pedicure without neglect, knowing that she was under her husband's scrutiny.

The years rolled on and Herbert and Florence were gifted with two children, a boy whom they named Robin and a girl called Nedra.

One would have thought that by now Herbert would relax his principles of isolationism and pursuit of the rich but nothing changed.

To him, life was a rulebook and the rules had to be adhered to but unfortunately he was the author of this book.

Nedra adored her father whom she believed to be "a self-made man." Little did she know how he acquired his wealth but it was quite evident that he was quite well off. His private car was the latest model Mercedes which he traded yearly for the newer model. He refurbished his house using the most expensive materials including the latest led technology. He even created an indoor swimming pool together with gym facilities. Plainly, he could do no more.

Robin, on the other hand, was taught that life was a rule-book and if you abided by the rules, you were bound to be successful. Life had to be strict and regimental and he bowed to his father's wishes in this respect.

As with everyone who was not beneficial, their cousins from the mother's side were also avoided, or, at best, ignored. Their parents were struggling and nor did they have any vocations from which Nedra and Robin could benefit. "Be courteous and polite, but avoid them when possible," Herbert reminded his children.

With the passing years, Herbert steadily progressed in the section of the company he worked for. In his job, he was conscientious and hardworking. He worked long hours, staying overtime and, at the same time, he made every effort to please his boss. For example, he would remember his boss's wife's birthday for whom he would buy a special card and a small present.

His boss realized how valuable Herbert was to the company. As a matter of fact, he was convinced that Herbert would be the key to his company's securing big projects that would make them big money instead of the peanut commissions that they were getting.

He, therefore, promoted Herbert and made him head to the export department. He increased his basic salary and the percentage of his commissions and he took personal care of him by inviting him and his wife to dinners, theatres, and operas.

"You are my right hand man" George assured Herbert privately. "I realize how hard you are working and if we secure the new project at hand, I promise to share the commission equally with you."

"I need something in writing and I need it to be certified by a solicitor," Herbert responded curtly. Herbert was reminded of his father's advice of not trusting anyone under any circumstance: 'Always secure yourself and never trust anyone. Always remember what I told you about the tongue being a piece of meat.'

"No problem," George answered. "I will prepare a letter to be certified by our solicitors but this is to remain private and confidential, just between you and me."

Herbert was ecstatic. The project was progressing favourably and was so big in scope, that should they win it, it would be "game over." It involved, among other things, the building of dams and bridges in the Middle East. Herbert's company was to assemble and coordinate the various expertise from the North American continent.

Ultimately, Herbert's company won the project. Actually "won" is not the correct word, as governmental heads supervising the project were complicit in the transaction, asking for big commissions. But what did Herbert and George care? As the project entailed billions of dollars, tens of millions of dollars which would go to Herbert and George was only a drop in a bucket. Herbert and George conferred and decided that their commissions should be paid to offshore accounts so as to avoid income tax.

Three years passed and the project was completed. Having received their commissions, their lifestyles changed. They became extravagant, leading lavish lifestyles. They bought the most expensive clothing and jewellery which they flaunted. A handbag, for example, would set them back a few thousand and a diamond bracelet tens of thousands. The onlookers in their social circles were sure to notice the display.

But everything that has an upside must, by nature's laws, have a downside. "It's like the wheel of fortune," a commoner in the renaissance might have remarked.

The funnelling of monies from abroad would surely catch the taxman's attention, as it did. An investigation was launched against Herbert and George and, as a result, they were both informed that they had to pay taxes on their undeclared profits or leave the country. Both decided to leave as the tax amount was substantial. So, they were given one week to leave.

On one hand, Florence felt dejected and crestfallen. How could she not accompany her husband? Perhaps she could visit him now and again, but that would not be the same. After all, he would be sacrificing a lot for her. He would have to leave his home on which he had spent so much and above all, he would have to leave his children and grandchildren around whom his world gravitated. This would mean separation or, at worst, a divorce.

On the other hand, she would venture into a world of freedom, a world which she only elicited in her subconscious. She would be free to do whatever she wanted without limits. She would not be controlled and dominated. No boss and no master. Herbert had been so restrictive that she had had to watch her every move when he was around. If a friend would call her, she would have to cut her conversation short with the words, "I'll call you later." Now she would be able to talk for hours to whomever she pleased. She could go to coffees, dinners, and even tours without being monitored. She could even have a part-time lover.

In case she would decide to live with Herbert, she would have to sell the house and their belongings and make periodic visits to her children and grandchildren but she would still remain in bondage. "Fuck that," she thought. Of course, there was the problem of gossippings and chatterings within her social circles, but she wouldn't care less. They would soon get over it.

Herbert was desperate to make arrangements for their departure. He was given one week to leave and, still believing that Florence would follow him, he decided to make the necessary arrangements and give the final instructions that evening.

That evening, Florence gathered all her courage to face Herbert and inform him of her decision.

"Herbert, before you start discussing the preparations we have to make, I want to tell you that I will not be coming with you. As a matter of fact, I have been thinking about our situation all week and I will be wanting a divorce."

"What?" Herbert was aghast. His scream resounded through the room. "I can't believe what I am hearing. Are you crazy? This is madness. You don't know what you are talking about."

"I have made my decision. I will not be travelling back and forth like a yoyo to see my children and grandchildren and at this stage in my life, I want to be physically and emotionally free. I am sure that we can make an amicable settlement."

"We have spent thirty years together. Do you want to throw that away?"

"It's the best option for both of us. You can start a new life without attachments and so can I. Of course, we will remain close friends as you are the father of our children. And so, the web of isolationism that you have built for thirty years has to break. You could be an Odysseus, free to build upon new experiences and adventures while I don't have to be a Penelope, living in anticipation.

Lightning Source UK Ltd.
Milton Keynes UK
UKOW03f0441050117
291435UK00003B/23/P